FALLING HARD

Also by Jessica Burkhart

The Saddlehill Academy series
Sweet & Bitter Rivals
The Showdown

The Canterwood Crest series

For older readers
Life Inside My Mind

For younger readers
The Unicorn Magic series

Saddlehill Academy

FALLING HARD

JESSICA BURKHART

Aladdin

New York   London   Toronto   Sydney   New Delhi

ALADDIN

An imprint of Simon & Schuster Children's Publishing Division
1230 Avenue of the Americas, New York, New York 10020
First Aladdin paperback edition March 2024
Text copyright © 2024 by Jessica Burkhart
Cover illustration copyright © 2024 by Lana Dudarenko
Cover filigree and crest by ProVectors/iStock
Cover horses by SvetlanaSoloveva/iStock
Also available in an Aladdin hardcover edition.
All rights reserved, including the right of reproduction in whole or in part in any form.
ALADDIN and related logo are registered trademarks of Simon & Schuster, LLC.
Simon & Schuster: Celebrating 100 Years of Publishing in 2024
For information about special discounts for bulk purchases, please contact
Simon & Schuster Special Sales at 1-866-506-1949 or business@simonandschuster.com.
The Simon & Schuster Speakers Bureau can bring authors to your live event.
For more information or to book an event contact the Simon & Schuster
Speakers Bureau at 1-866-248-3049 or visit our website at www.simonspeakers.com.
Cover designed by Karin Paprocki
Interior designed by Mike Rosamilia
The text of this book was set in Adobe Garamond Pro.
Manufactured in the United States of America 0224 OFF
2 4 6 8 10 9 7 5 3 1
Library of Congress Control Number 2023940686
ISBN 9781665912990 (hc)
ISBN 9781665912976 (pbk)
ISBN 9781665913003 (ebook)

To all my readers—my Harts—thank you
for sticking with me!

We're Going Where?!

AS I RODE BEAU INTO THE ARENA FOR practice, I couldn't wait for Rebecca, my riding instructor, to get here. She had *two* big announcements to make, and guesses were already running wild as to what those could be.

With the way things were, I needed something to look forward to. It had been a couple of weeks since I'd confessed the Selly secret to everyone in Rebecca's office. That secret? Oof. Last year, I'd accidentally written the wrong start time for a show class on a whiteboard, not catching my mistake.

And as a result, Selly had missed her class and Rebecca had taken her out of the running for team captain because of it. Because of *me*.

Once she'd found out what I'd done, Selly had grabbed me in the stable and promised to ruin my life. If that hadn't been enough, I'd barely seen my best friends because they were always busy. But all I could do was keep going and hope that things would settle down soon . . . if Selly didn't take me out first.

The rest of my Interscholastic Pony League teammates— Keir, Selly, Nina, Emery, and Thea—trickled in on their horses. We all competed in Area 1 for Foxbury, and Rebecca had grouped us by skill level.

Once my stepsister, Emery, had joined us this year, we'd been split into two smaller competition teams. Keir captained the first team, which was made up of Selly, Emery, and Keir. The second team was Thea, Nina, and me, with Thea as our team captain.

As we finished warming up, Rebecca walked into the arena and motioned for us to ride over to her. My teammates and I lined up our horses in front of her, the anticipation making me shift around in the saddle.

"Before we start the lesson, I have two announcements," Rebecca said. "First, our next show date is finalized, and we have a lovely host stable."

Everyone glanced at each other before looking at Rebecca. This was the news we'd been waiting for!

"We'll be having a Haunted Halloween Classic," Rebecca said. "Complete with a costume contest, decor, and scary-themed jumps. Of course, it'll count for points, but it's also about having fun and showing off your creativity."

"Where?" Keir asked. "Here?"

"I heard someone say Millford Stables," Nina said, excitement rising in her voice.

Rebecca shook her head. "Nope, not here, and not at Millford." She grinned. "We'll be going to Connecticut, to a little place called Canterwood Crest Academy."

"WHAT?!" I shrieked.

Everyone broke out in excited cheers, and Thea reached over and squeezed my forearm so hard, I was sure she'd leave fingerprint-shaped bruises.

"We're going to Canterwood? For real? This isn't a trick?" Selly asked.

"It's too early in October for tricks," Rebecca said. "We'll be spending a few nights near their campus. They're hosting a rider get-together the night before the comp starts."

"When?" I asked, barely breathing.

"The weekend before Halloween," Rebecca said. "So, start planning your costumes!"

I grinned at Thea. This was the best treat ever!

"And my other announcement is about Sasha Silver and Heather Fox's winter clinic," Rebecca said. "I know many of you plan to apply, right?"

Everyone nodded.

"Great! The application requires a video showcasing your riding talent, so we'll film those this week."

This was almost too much to process! How were we supposed to focus on riding after those announcements?

"All right. Let's quickly run down today's plan!" Rebecca snapped back into business mode. "We're going to work on dressage, starting with looseness. I want to see softening throughout your horses' bodies, because I've noticed some horses are looking a little stiff. We're going to do some transitions from a working walk to a slow trot, and then we'll transition back to a walk. And once you start a new transition, I want you to make a figure eight. Clear?"

"Clear!" we confirmed.

"In a moment, you'll walk your horses for ten strides, then transition to a slow trot," Rebecca said. "You'll trot for four or five strides, then drop back to a walk and make a figure eight. Then repeat. We'll do this for two rounds in this direction before switching to counterclockwise."

I nodded. Beau and I could do this.

"This exercise should help your horses by making their transitions much more seamless," Rebecca added. "Everyone spread out at a walk."

I let Beau fall into line behind Chaos and Thea, and we went to the arena rail. Beau, nicely warmed up, moved smoothly and quietly while awaiting my next command.

"Starting now, count ten strides, then trot," Rebecca called to us, "and the exercise will begin."

In my head, I counted Beau's strides as we walked down the rail. When I hit *ten*, I squeezed my legs against his sides and asked for a trot to start a figure eight. It took him a bit too long to respond, and it wasn't as immediate as I would have liked, so I added more leg. *This exercise is perfect for us,* I thought.

After five strides at a trot, I asked him to walk. He playfully tossed his head, tugging on the reins and trying to keep trotting. But I sat deeper in the saddle and let him know I meant what I'd asked for: it was time to walk.

Beau slowed, finally, and then we repeated the transitions exercise. This go-round, his responses were much faster, and I scratched his withers to let him know he'd done great.

Dressage was my weakest area. We competed in three-day eventing, so we did dressage, show jumping, and cross-country. I was a huge fan of jumping, and soaring into the air never became less of a thrill. Everything about jumping was exciting and pulse-pounding to me, and while I'd thought about only concentrating on those areas, I knew myself and my riding. Beau and I needed the dressage work to help keep our working partnership at its strongest.

Three-day eventing pushed both of us to be our very best, from the delicate dance of dressage to the speed of show jumping to the boldness of cross-country. And those three phases blended to create one giant challenge. It was the best, most exciting thing I'd ever done.

My attention wandered, though, as I thought about the Canterwood show. The place where Sasha Silver and Lauren Towers took off.

"Abby!" Rebecca yelled. "How long have you been trotting?"

I snapped out of my daydream. *Whoops.* I was halfway down the arena and hadn't been counting any strides. Cringing, I hurried to slow Beau to a walk as I burned from embarrassment at being called out.

"Pay attention, people," Rebecca said. "I need you all to be focused on counting strides and making the transitions. Or we're going to be here all day."

Behind me, Selly snickered, but I kept my attention on Beau. We worked our way from a walk to a trot and back again.

We did the exercise going counterclockwise a few times before Rebecca called us over to line up in front of her.

"Let's get right into pairs work," Rebecca said. "Abby and Emery, we'll put you together." Rebecca smiled at Emery and me. "Then Nina and Keir, and Selly and Thea. You're partners for the rest of the lesson."

My stomach sank.

After everything that had gone down, I didn't want to work with Emery. After all, she'd hid Nina's identity as the Truth X. Poser from me. Nina had done so much damage. Clenching my teeth, I fought to keep an annoyed expression off my face. It was enough that we had lessons together, but being Emery's actual partner? Ugh.

I knew without looking at my teammates that Thea and Selly couldn't be happy about their pairing either. But Rebecca had warned Thea that one more mistake would cost her the spot as our team's captain, so I was certain my best friend wasn't going to complain about being partnered with Selly even if she wanted to.

"With your partner, spread out in the arena and find a spot for the two of you," Rebecca said. "You're going to coach each other through a couple of leg yields. Do this first at a walk, then a trot. I'll be watching and offering support if you need it, but I want to see you and your partner give each other instruction. You need to talk about why you're doing leg yields and what we can use them for. Got it?"

"Got it," I mumbled.

Everyone else nodded.

Leg yields meant moving your horse forward and sideways and asking the horse to cross their inside legs in front of their outside legs. While doing this, the horse kept their body straight except for flexing at the poll, and the horse's jaw pointed in the opposite direction.

"Grab your partner and get started," Rebecca said.

I started Beau past Selly and her mare, Ember, and Selly caught my eye. "You look like you're going to cry, Abby," she whispered.

"I'm not."

Selly smirked. "We'll see." She turned to Emery and gave her a little wave. "Have fun, Em!"

I clenched my teeth. I hated every second of this, but I was not going to give them the satisfaction. And I wasn't giving Rebecca even the tiniest reason to call me out.

"Let's go," I said to Emery.

Her hazel eyes were wide as she looked from Selly to me before finally nodding. "Want to go over there?" She pointed to a spot on the rail a few yards down in the arena.

"Yep." My tone was brisk and cool. We were going to smash these leg yields and get this over with as quickly as possible.

"Abby, please," Emery said. "I know you don't want to talk to me, and I get it, but we have to make this work in the arena. I don't want to get in trouble."

I glared at her. "Neither do I. And I'm talking to you, aren't I?"

"Fine," Emery said. "Let's get through this."

Sister vs. Sister

IN SILENCE, WE RODE AWAY FROM THE other teams so that everyone had enough space. Beau and Bliss, oblivious to what was going on between Emery and me, walked happily beside each other. For a second, I wished I could go back in time. Back before I'd been so burned by Emery. Back before my dad had married her mom. Back before I'd ever known she existed.

We reached our spot on the rail, and I halted Beau. Emery pulled up Bliss beside him. I took a deep breath. *Just get through this,* I told myself. I could go back to not speaking to Emery ever again the second this was done.

"So, why are we doing leg yields?" I asked, trying to keep the bite out of my tone.

"They're supposed to help the rider with different aids," Emery said. "They teach your horse to be responsive and understand what you're asking for."

I nodded. "They also help keep your horse supple and loose."

"Thankfully, they're not required on our dressage test."

"Yet," I said.

"Right. Yet. I'm not super good at them, but I know we need them to do more advanced moves."

It was a bit of a relief that they weren't expected from us at this level. It gave me time to keep learning and perfecting the move before I had to do it in a competition, when stress levels were high.

"Want to go first?" I asked. "Maybe do a ten-meter half circle to set you up for it?"

"Sure, that sounds good."

And without a second of hesitation, Emery urged Bliss forward, ahead of Beau and me. She walked Bliss down the rail, and at the corner, turned her in a half circle, then asked for a leg yield. Bliss hesitated for a second. I could almost see her thinking about what to do, but then she yielded to Emery's cues and moved sideways and forward at the same time.

"Nice!" I called, unable to help myself. Plus, I knew Rebecca was watching, and I didn't want her to catch me being unsupportive of Emery.

Emery smiled as she let Bliss out of the leg yield and walked her straight toward Beau and me. "Thanks!"

"Maybe you should do it at a trot now," I suggested. "Bliss might be in the right headspace to try again. Then Beau and I can go."

"That works for me."

"Make sure you keep your shoulders square with hers," I said.

Emery nodded. "Good tip. Thanks!"

She asked Bliss to trot, and they headed down the rail and started to make their ten-meter half circle. This time, as Emery asked Bliss to leg yield, she kept her shoulders in the correct position, and she carried both hands slightly to the outside. This kept the bit even in Bliss's mouth.

There was zero hesitation from Bliss this time. The mare

moved quickly and easily in a beautiful leg yield, coming toward Beau and me while going sideways.

"You got it!" I called.

Out of the corner of my eye, Rebecca walked closer to watch Emery. Our instructor had a giant smile on her face as she scribbled something on her iPad.

After a few strides, Emery relaxed and let Bliss trot straight forward. Her smile was as wide as Rebecca's as she eased Bliss to a walk and then patted the mare's glossy shoulder.

"Good job, girl!" Emery told her.

Bliss snorted, shaking her head and sending her forelock flying. The mare was proud of what she'd done.

"That was . . . really good," I said.

"Thanks! I know Bliss has probably done it a thousand times with her old owner, but it's still fairly new to me. She teaches me stuff all the time."

"I know that feeling."

Beau was very much like Bliss in that regard, although he was greener than she was. Still, he'd competed in the IPL before I'd gotten him, so he had come to me with some experience.

Now it was my turn.

I set Beau off at a brisk walk down the rail, and as he walked, I decided I wanted to try the leg yield without going into a circle first. We came to the corner, and I turned Beau around to face Emery and Bliss. As we went back to the rail, I saw the confusion on Emery's face.

It was time to go for it.

I put a little more weight on my inside seat bone and brought my outside leg back behind the girth. I could use it as a driving aid and a way to keep Beau's haunches from swinging out.

Then I moved my inside left behind the girth and started to push Beau sideways and away from the rail.

I asked Beau to bend his head, just enough so I could see his inside nostril, and I held my breath.

He. Responded. Immediately.

Beau swung to the side, leg yielding as I'd asked, and I tried to keep my hands from shaking with excitement. We were doing a leg yield without coming out of a half circle first! We'd only done this once before!

I kept up the pressure with my inside leg to keep Beau moving forward and sideways for a few more strides before I let him straighten and walk forward.

Emery's mouth was slightly open as she stared at us, her eyes wide.

"ABBY ST. CLAIR!" I whipped my head over my shoulder to see Rebecca, eyes glued to us. "That was beautiful!"

My heart thudded in my chest. I could count on one hand the number of times Rebecca had cheered at me like that during a lesson.

"Thank you!" I called back, grinning as I leaned down to pat Beau's neck.

"That was so good," Emery said when we reached her. "You didn't even need the half circle."

And for a split second, I almost forgot about what she'd done. And how I didn't want to even look at her. I was so beyond excited. But then it all came rushing back.

"Thanks," I said. "I was going to do the half circle too, but then I went for it and tried it this way. Honestly, I wasn't expecting him to do it. I thought for sure we'd have to go back and try again."

"Now you've got to do it at a trot," Emery said.

"Everyone, pause!" Rebecca called. "Except Abby. I want you all to watch Abby and Beau for a minute."

Six pairs of eyes watched us.

"We got this," I whispered to Beau.

I turned him away from Emery and Bliss and then asked him to trot.

We made our turn at the corner of the arena, and once we were a few strides down, I asked him for a leg yield.

And Beau, my heart horse, the horse of my dreams, and my angel, did a flawless leg yield at a trot.

We were rocking this!

When I pulled him up, Rebecca led everyone in a round of applause. Everyone except for Nina and Selly, of course, who fake-clapped while looking as if they'd eaten a sour candy. But I didn't care.

Beau and I had just done *that*!

I Don't Like the Odds

AFTER MY LESSON YESTERDAY, I FELL into bed early, all smiley from a great ride. But this morning anxiety woke me up, and I rolled over in bed, struggling to take a deep breath. It was barely five a.m., and across our room, Vivi was sound asleep.

Waking up breathless with anxiety crushing my chest was something I'd been dealing with since Mom left when I was seven. When I was younger, I was terrified that I'd wake up and find Dad gone too, and I'd be all alone. Sometimes I'd get up in the middle of the night and poke my head into my dad's bedroom to make sure he was still there. It had gotten so bad for a while that I'd slept in the hallway outside his room, so I'd know if he left.

That's when he'd taken me to a therapist, and I'd gotten help. Now I didn't have as many panic attacks, but I still struggled with anxiety. I tried to remind myself that Dad and I were great, and he'd really been making an effort to be there for me after the disaster that was my last show. But I hadn't been worrying about him tonight—it was all about Vivi and Thea.

After staring at the ceiling and getting more and more jittery, I threw back my covers and put on sweats. Maybe a run would help me clear my head.

I left the coziness of Amherst and stepped into the mildly chilly air, walking down the sidewalk toward the river. There was no one else out at this hour, and I relished the quiet of campus.

Once I was warmed up, I started jogging along the scenic path. But thoughts of Selly coming after me kept swirling around in my brain. I picked up the pace and pushed myself, running until the only thing I could think about was breathing and listening to the sounds of my shoes on the pavement.

I hadn't jogged in so long! After school, I was either riding Beau or teaching Arden, the younger rider I'd been assigned by Rebecca. Working with her had eaten away any free time I'd had, but it had been part of the deal Rebecca had made with me, Selly, Nina, and Thea to allow us to stay on the riding team.

When I made it back to my room, I showered and got ready for school. The run had helped a bit, but sitting still felt impossible. I needed to lean on my friends and talk to them instead of keeping everything in.

But instead, I kept messing with my plants and watering them when they definitely didn't need a drink. They were going to drown, for sure.

"I'm staying over at Pia's tonight," Vivi said. "I think I told you that already, though."

"Oh," I mumbled. She hadn't told me. "Cool! Have fun."

Pia was one of Vivi's friends from theater class. Usually we didn't sleep over in other houses except on the weekends. But it felt like Vivi couldn't wait to get out of our room.

She and Thea had sworn they'd both understood why I'd kept the Selly secret, and things were fine between us when we were actually spending time together. But that had been so rare over the last couple of weeks that I couldn't help but worry that I'd done something else to make them not want to hang with me.

I wanted to ask Vivi if she was free this weekend, but it seemed like she was good without me. So I just gave her an awkward wave as she headed for the door.

"See you in class," Vivi said. And before I could even reply, she was out the door.

"Yeah, see you in class," I said to no one.

I turned my bunny ears cactus to get the sun on a different side, then glanced at my phone. I still had time to kill before I left for class.

With a sigh, I grabbed my iPad and plopped down on my bed. I typed in Sasha Silver's website address and browsed the pages that had info on all her big wins, where she was going next, and photos of her with Charm and Sterling Silver. In a recent pic, she was bareback on Charm, grinning and holding Sterling's lead line. Both horses looked toward the camera with pricked ears. They'd come such a long way since Sasha's Canterwood Crest days.

Then I tapped on "Clinics and Workshops" and found what I was looking for.

Winter Clinic Hosted by
Sasha Silver and Heather Fox,

December 27–January 3

Come join Sasha and Heather for an unforgettable week of intensive riding and training. Improve your riding and horsemanship during this clinic with two decorated equestrians.

Applications are now open for a limited number of spots. Anyone wishing to apply must submit an audition video of their strengths as a rider as well as a letter about what they wish to accomplish here.

Last year there were over three thousand applicants, and we regret we could only offer spots to a dozen Interscholastic Pony League riders and ten adult riders. This year, we expect even more applications, but we will cap this clinic at those same numbers to allow for individual attention.

Guidelines for your video and letter are below. The deadline is November 1. Looking forward to seeing your audition!

—Sasha and Heather

My mouth went dry. Three thousand applicants? Those odds were . . . Not Good. Especially since I had a feeling that everyone at Foxbury would apply, and there were way better riders than me.

But that just meant my audition video had to sparkle—it had to show Sasha and Heather how much I wanted this. I turned off my iPad and stood, pushing my shoulders back.

"I'm letting go of everything that's going on," I told my plants, "and I'm going to make the best audition video that Sasha and Heather have ever seen."

That would give me something to focus on besides ping-ponging between wondering what was up with Vivi and Thea and freaking out about Selly.

Slowly I gathered my notebooks and textbooks for class and slung my backpack over my shoulder.

I swiped my phone off my desk and texted Mila, the new girl at Foxbury. The *cute* new girl at Foxbury. We'd talked a lot after that awful day in Rebecca's office, and she'd been so supportive and understanding.

Abby: Are you applying to Sasha Silver and Heather Fox's winter riding clinic?

She wrote me back right away.

Mila: Yesss! Are you?

Abby: Definitely! And yay, I hope we both get in! ☺

Mila: Me too!

But as I looked at the texts from Mila, I couldn't help but worry if I should even be her friend. My own best friends were being weird around me. What if Mila ended up being like that too?

Mila texted again: What are you up to?

That time, I left her on read.

And ... Action!

ON WEDNESDAY, I WAS SO READY TO ride Beau later. Working with him always helped me get out of my head.

Classes let out early for a teacher workshop, and I headed toward the cafeteria for lunch. Just across the quad, Thea and Vivi meandered down the sidewalk together. I figured they would go into the caf, but instead, they kept walking.

I hurried to catch up to them.

"Thea! Vivi!" I called.

They turned around, trading quick glances with each other.

"Want to get lunch together?" I asked. "I don't feel like cafeteria food. Maybe McDonald's?"

"We kind of already have lunch plans," Thea said. She played with the hem of her shirt, scrunching the fabric with her fingers.

"Sorry, Abs," Vivi said. "But we can have lunch together tomorrow!"

My face burned as I looked at them. They'd never not wanted me to have lunch with them. And *plans*? Like, plans for lunch together or with someone else? I had so many questions.

"Oh, no big deal," I chirped. "I'll see you later."

Even though it was the biggest of deals.

"Definitely!" Vivi said, smiling at me like this was totally fine and normal before she and Thea went on their way.

Fine. I would walk to the McDonald's right on the edge of campus and have the best solo lunch ever.

After a tasty lunch of chicken nuggets and fries, I got ready for riding and headed to the stable. Seeing Beau always helped my mood, though, and the moment I threw my arms around his neck and breathed in his horsey scent, I felt a little better.

"Let's get you groomed and ready," I told him. "It's lesson day."

As I groomed him and tacked him up, I laughed to myself when I started to think about explaining what I was doing as I was doing it.

"I've been working with Arden so much that I almost wanted to talk myself through how to groom you," I said to Beau. "Whoops."

Beau dozed on and off while I got him ready, and after I fastened the chin strap on my helmet, I led him outside. Rebecca had group texted us to meet in the biggest outdoor arena, which was closest to the stable.

Beau pricked his ears forward as we walked, tugging on the reins. As I turned him in the opposite direction, my eye caught on Mila climbing up on the fence to sit and watch our lesson.

Smiling, she waved at me, and I awkwardly waved back, then adjusted my reins. This was probably our last week before Mila joined our riding team, because her test was this weekend. I felt bad for not texting her back yesterday, but my head was spinning from trying to figure out what was going on with Thea and Vivi.

The rest of my team came into the arena, and I let out a small sigh of relief that I'd managed to warm up without having to talk to anyone. Rebecca walked into the arena, all smiles, as she waved for us to bring our horses in front of her.

"Good afternoon, everyone!" she said. "As you know, you need an audition video to submit to the winter clinic that shows off a bit of your flatwork and a little of your jumping. That's what we're doing today and tomorrow with our lesson groups."

I grinned, unable to stop myself from looking at Thea with wide eyes.

"We're filming *today*?" I asked.

"Yup," Rebecca said. "Allie is free, so she's kindly going to pop in and film each of you for a couple of minutes. She'll upload the footage and send you the link whenever you're ready."

Allie was one of Foxbury's other instructors.

Selly raised her hand, frowning. "I didn't wear my good breeches, though," she said after Rebecca called on her. "I don't want to look grubby on my tape."

"You look fine." Rebecca waved her hand in the air. "This

isn't a show. It's practice. And you're in practice clothes, along with everyone else."

"I guess," Selly said. But she swiped furiously at her breeches with one hand and smoothed her maroon T-shirt with the other. I understood where she was coming from, though. If I'd known we were going to film today, I would have brushed my hair before I'd left Saddlehill and maybe put on some lip gloss.

"First we'll run through a trot/canter transition exercise," Rebecca said, "and then we'll jump. I want to see everyone riding their very best. But try not to get nervous. Remember, this will not be anything new. It's a regular riding lesson. You're showing Sasha and Heather what you can do comfortably at your current riding level."

I swallowed. Hard.

I'd watched Sasha compete for years and years. Heather, too. And I'd dreamed about Sasha watching me ride, thinking the opportunity to ride in front of her might never come. This winter clinic application would give me a chance to show her a few precious moments of my skills. But . . . what if she wasn't impressed? The thought sent shivers up and down my arms. *Maybe she* will *be impressed with you,* I told myself. That was all I could hope for, honestly—for her to see me and Beau and think we were worthy of her time and energy.

Now I was glad Rebecca hadn't given us a heads-up about today. If I'd known, I would have done nothing but panic. I pushed my shoulders back and tried to put on my game face.

"Ready?" Rebecca asked.

"Ready!" I said with everyone else.

Beau the Brat

REBECCA WALKED US THROUGH THE trot-canter-trot exercise we'd be doing, while Allie, with her phone in hand, came into the arena and stood ready to film us.

"Everyone spread out, and when you hit marker A, start making a large circle at a working trot," Rebecca said. "I want to see nice forward motion from your horses!"

We were all down by C, so I started Beau at a working trot, and we followed Thea and Chaos toward A.

At A, I sat deep in the saddle and asked Beau for a canter

on his right lead. He bounded into a smooth canter, and I maintained a safe distance between us and Chaos. I kept my right leg at the girth to make Beau's right hind leg reach farther forward, bending as I held him on the left rein.

"More right rein, Abby!" Rebecca called.

I did as she asked, and Beau showed more right flexion at his poll. Whew!

"Your left leg needs to be behind the girth, Selly," Rebecca said. "Ember is swinging too far left."

I kept my eyes focused between Beau's ears, trying not to listen to all the critiques my teammates were getting. The only thing I needed to focus on was Beau.

"When you hit A, bring them to a trot," Rebecca said, "and circle again."

As Beau cantered the last half of our circle, I made sure to apply forward pressure with both seat bones. All I wanted to do was make Beau shine!

At A, I did a half halt and stilled my seat, asking him for a trot. I kept my inside long and closed my hands on the reins.

Ahead of us, Thea had asked Chaos for a trot, but the gelding had charged past A still at a canter.

Beau wanted to keep pace with his buddy, and he tugged

on the reins, tossing his head when I asked for a trot. But I stayed firm, my hands and seat telling him we were going to trot and not canter anymore. A few strides past A, he listened and slowed to a hurried trot. But still a trot!

"Good work, Abby," Rebecca said from her spot in the middle of our circle. "You handled that well."

I flashed her a smile of thanks. Allie joined Rebecca, peering at her phone as she filmed.

I tried not to let my thoughts run wild, but they became a constant thread of *OMG, SASHA SILVER IS GOING TO SEE THIS!!!* and *OMG, HEATHER FOX WILL BE WATCHING!!!!* With endless exclamation points, of course.

"After you finish a circle at a trot," Rebecca said, "trot down the rail to C and repeat the circle exercises, going in the same direction."

While Beau and I completed our circle, I tried to push all the thoughts of the Canterwood graduates out of my head. I had to stay focused on what I was doing, or it would show in my audition, and I'd never get an invitation to the winter clinic. And that invite was something I wanted more than *anything*.

"Keir, get your lower leg under your seat and remember

your other cues," Rebecca advised. "Magic's got a hollow back."

I let Beau out of the circle and pointed him toward the rail so we could head down to C. As we headed for the rail, I caught a glimpse of Emery and Bliss. Emery was in the zone—lips pressed together, eyes focused between Bliss's ears, and posture relaxed.

I tore my gaze away from her and tried to focus on my ride. But my mind wandered. Maybe Sasha and Heather would watch my audition and think Beau and I made a great team. In my imagination, it all played out in front of me: Sasha watching my submission, all smiles, sending me the fastest acceptance email ever and telling me she couldn't wait to work with Beau and me. This was going to be the best audition she'd ever seen! I was going to—

NO!

Before I could react, Beau shied, ducked his head, and bucked playfully. He caught me so off guard, and I was so lost in my daydream, that my reaction time was too slow! Before I could even grab for his mane or try to sit it out, I flew out of the saddle and soared through the air before—

WHAM!

The breath got knocked right out of me as I slammed into

the dirt, curled up so I didn't land on an arm or leg. My left shoulder took the brunt of the fall, and I gasped as I tried to take a breath.

Ouch. I couldn't believe this! I'd really fallen off right now?

"Abby!"

Rebecca's voice floated toward me. I sat up, holding out one of my hands. "I'm—I'm okay!"

And I was okay, physically—I'd just had the wind knocked out of me. It wasn't the first time I'd fallen—not even close. But it took everything in me not to burst into tears. Not because I was hurt, but because Allie was filming! I'd ruined my audition tape! There was no way I could send that to Sasha and Heather.

Beau stood a few feet away, head down and not looking at me. He felt bad already, I could tell. Tears blurred my vision, and I swiped them away. I didn't want Selly, Nina, and Emery to see me cry.

I especially didn't want to think about Emery right now. On top of everything, she'd looked spectacular every time I'd sneaked a look in her direction. What if she got into the clinic too? Or . . . I froze in horror. What if she got a spot and I didn't?

Rebecca hurried over as I stood on shaky legs and brushed

the dirt off my breeches. The action gave me something to do, something to pull me out of my head and my panic over the audition.

"That was a hard fall," she said, her worried eyes sweeping over me. "You sure you're okay?"

"I'm fine." I sniffled, holding back a sob as I glanced at Allie. "But—"

"Abby, don't even worry about it!" Allie called, waving her free hand at me. "You can edit it right out. I got great footage of your flatwork before that."

"See?" Rebecca said. She patted my forearm. "As long as you're okay, let's get you back on Beau."

I managed a deep breath this time, nodding. "Okay." Beau, head still down, trained a wary eye on me as I walked over to him. "You got that out of your system, huh? Ready to get back to work?"

He sniffed my hands, bobbing his head ever so slightly as if to say, *Yes*.

Rebecca gave me a leg up, and I righted myself in the saddle. Now that I was up, the rest of my teammates who kept their horses at the other end of the arena started heading my way.

I let Beau follow Nina's gray gelding, Adore, and Selly and Ember wound up behind me. I wasn't going to let it bother me, though, being sandwiched between those two. Instead, I would make sure every second of my audition sparkled from here on out.

No matter what.

I kept Beau at an even trot as he moved toward the C marker. But as we went into our large circle to the right, Ember's hoofbeats got closer and closer.

"Abby, come on!" Selly said to my back. "You're going too slow."

I wasn't. At all.

I shook my head, keeping Beau at a steady working trot.

Behind us, Selly let Ember edge up to Beau, and I could sense how close they were.

"Go around, then," I said through gritted teeth.

But she didn't. Instead, Selly kept speeding up and slowing down, backing Ember on and off and crowding Beau. Rebecca was busy talking to Thea and currently too preoccupied to pay much attention to me and Selly.

Beau got a little grumpy and flattened his ears a bit as Ember continued to get way too close. He wasn't a kicker, and

Selly knew that, or she'd never let Ember get up in his business so much.

"Selly!" Rebecca called, watching us now that she was finished with Thea. "Watch your distance, please!"

"I'm trying," she said, "but it's so hard when Abby's riding like this!"

Riding like *this*? She was the one messing up the spacing and letting Ember crowd Beau!

Still, I didn't want to whine about it. Not now. Not when Allie was trying to film, and we were all already on probation with Rebecca.

Selly was . . . *bold* for trying this. But that was part of her game—she pushed it as hard as she could without letting the adults see what she was doing. If they noticed, she pretended to be innocent and blamed it on someone else.

Rebecca walked over to stand in the center of our circle. She had been an instructor long enough that most days, she had eyes on everyone. But once in a while, she couldn't watch every one of us all at once.

"If Abby isn't keeping pace, then you can go around her, Selly," Rebecca said. "But don't let Ember get so up on Beau."

With that, Selly trotted Ember up to Beau and me, keeping

even with us until we'd passed Allie. Then she let Ember canter, and they slid in front of us. She'd stayed even with me long enough to block us in front of the camera as we'd ridden by.

I rolled my eyes. Whatever! Allie had said she already had plenty of good footage of Beau and me. Selly could try to block us all she wanted. Surely it would be obvious on camera what she was doing. Right?

I'd been so focused on her and Ember passing me that I'd trotted another half circle when I was supposed to be cantering. I waited until Beau and I hit C again, then I asked him for a canter. He moved smoothly under me, listening to me and moving with solid impulsion.

We finished our flatwork with no more hiccups. Then, while Allie and Rebecca set up a couple of verticals and an oxer, we rode a short practice course.

"Allie's going to film each of you riding this minicourse," Rebecca said. "You'll ride it once. Start with the verticals and end with the oxer." She raised an eyebrow. "Got it?"

"Got it," I said with everyone else.

"Good. For the jumping order, I want Keir to kick us off. Then let's have Selly, Nina, Thea, Emery, and, last but not least, Abby."

I winced a little. Going last meant I had to watch everyone else ride before me. It also gave me that much more time to get nervous. Usually, I didn't get anxious about jumping, especially during practice. But hello, this was a big deal! No, it was a *huge* deal. The hugest of deals.

My teammates and I, minus Keir, walked our horses out of the way of the jump course, where we could still keep the horses moving before their turns. Allie stood off to the side near the oxer, where she had a clear view of all the jumps. It was a basic, straightforward course, but as Beau's earlier buck had proved, anything could happen.

"Ready when you are!" Allie told Keir.

He eased his chestnut gelding, Magic, away from us before urging him into a trot, then a slow canter. Keir was the least experienced rider on our team, but he was a hard worker. And I couldn't imagine shows without him. He was the glue of the team. He'd gotten together with Thea to call the group meeting when everything had gone so, so sideways at the last show. Keir was a consummate professional, and I wished I had his levelheadedness.

With ease, he guided Magic over the jumps, the gelding's tail streaming in the air behind him as he landed on the other side of the oxer.

"Beautiful, Keir!" Rebecca said, clapping. "That'll look great on your audition."

Grinning, Keir said, "Thank you!"

"Selly, you're up," Rebecca said. She nodded at her and then focused on scribbling notes on her iPad. I wished I could see those notes!

Or maybe not, since they probably had criticism that I didn't need to see about my riding from past lessons.

Selly, next to me, caught my eye. "You're going to wish you'd never heard about the clinic," she whispered.

I started to ask what she meant, but the evil glint in her eye made me stop.

"It'll crush you when I make it and you don't," she added.

Before I could say anything, she urged Ember forward and away from Beau and me.

Gimme All the
Lucky Charms

RITTING MY TEETH, I WATCHED SELLY bring Ember to a canter and point her at the first vertical. Everything about the way Selly handled her dark bay mare was smooth. She looked as though she melted into Ember's back, making them one. I couldn't help but feel a wave of panic. Selly always rode well, but this was some next-level stuff. As much as she was a fan of Jasmine King—an old classmate of Sasha's with a notoriously risky riding style—and not so much Sasha, I knew this was all to impress Sasha and Heather and get into the clinic.

"They look . . . ," Thea whispered.

". . . amazing," I finished.

This. Was. Not. Good.

After they finished, Selly eased Ember into a half circle. When she faced us, the grin on her face said it all.

"Selly, *wow*!" Rebecca said. She shook her head, trying to take it all in. "That was a brilliant ride! I'm so proud. I don't see how Sasha and Heather won't be impressed."

Ugh. That last sentence was so not what I wanted to hear.

It cranked up the pressure on me not only to do well but to do amazing. And after the lesson Beau and I'd had so far? I wasn't sure if we had amazing in us today.

While Nina and Thea did equally fantastic rounds, I pep-talked myself. *Find your awesome. You know you're capable of it!*

Then it was Emery's turn.

"Go, Em!" Selly cheered.

"Yeah, get it, Emery!" Nina added.

I didn't say a word. This was something I wanted for myself. Something to do *by* myself. Well, without Emery, any-way. She was a great rider, though, so I figured the chances of her not getting an invite were slim. Or maybe none of us would get one! My thoughts ran wild. What if Sasha and Heather picked Ava and Olivia—the current Canterwood superstars who would surely apply to the clinic? Then there would be two fewer spots. And maybe they'd pick lots of riders from other schools and leave no spots for us.

Stop, stop, I told myself. *You have no idea what's going to happen.*

Worrying about it wasn't going to change anything—my brain knew it, but getting my heart to accept it wasn't easy. I needed to have the best ride ever, and my need for a perfect ride only increased as Emery and Bliss had a flawless round.

"Yaaay, Emery!" Selly cheered.

Rebecca applauded, and I couldn't help but join in. No matter what my feelings were toward Emery, she and Bliss deserved the applause.

There was no way Sasha and Heather wouldn't pick her. Not after a ride like that.

"Emery, you should be very proud," Rebecca said. "You and Bliss looked great, and I'm so pleased with how you're doing on our team."

Emery smiled, leaning down to pat Bliss's neck. "Thank you! I'm learning so much here."

"And it shows," Rebecca said. She looked over at me, then nodded. "All right, Abby. Close it out for today."

You can do this, I told myself. *It's three jumps.*

I rolled my shoulders, then pushed them back and tilted my chin up. I could do this. *We* could do this.

With that, I asked Beau for a trot. Once we were away from the group, I sat deep in the saddle and urged him into a nice canter. This time, Beau had 100 percent of my focus. I shoved all thoughts of Selly and Emery out of my mind, thinking only about the ride.

These three jumps were going to be perfect.

After Beau and I made a half circle, I lined him up along the rail and pointed him at the first vertical. His hoofbeats pounded in my ears, and I lost myself in their rhythm.

I forgot about Sasha.

And Heather.

And my teammates.

Instead, I felt the moment and started counting down in my head for liftoff.

Three strides . . . two, one, now!

On *now*, I rose out of the saddle and pushed my hands up along Beau's neck as he lifted off the ground. He caught the perfect amount of air, sailing over the jump poles and landing easily on the other side.

One down, two to go!

I guided Beau toward the second jump—the other vertical. Ears pointed forward, he cantered toward it, and he went up in the air at just the right second. I wished I could suspend time so we could stay like this! But all too soon, his hooves touched the arena dirt.

Yes, we're doing it!

One more, boy, I wanted to tell him. *One! More!*

I did a half halt because I wanted to make sure Beau was paying as much attention to me as possible between now and the oxer. It had a good spread, so the timing of our takeoff and landing was more crucial than ever. Beau responded favorably, deepening his hind-leg step, and I felt him shift down. *Excellent.*

We cantered at an even pace toward the oxer, and a perfectly balanced Beau was gathered neatly under me. He cantered up to the poles, and at exactly the right second, he launched into the air as I lifted into the two-point position, moving my hands up along Beau's neck. As he soared over the oxer, I smiled. I couldn't help it! This was such a good jump!

Beau landed like a pro on the other side of the oxer, and

I adjusted my seat to sit back down in the saddle. We hadn't even come close to tapping the top rail.

"Great job, boy!" I told him, leaning down to pat his neck. "You did it!" Beau flexed his neck as I petted him. He knew how well he'd done. "I'm so proud of you!"

He shook his head, sending his mane flying as he cantered with a frisky bounce in his step. Laughing, I patted his neck again. I eased him into a large half circle as we turned around to face my teammates.

"Way to go, Abs!" Keir cheered.

I grinned at him before glancing at Thea. Normally, she was the first to cheer for me. But she was looking toward the nearby arena, where some of the younger riders, including Thea's sister, Cora, trotted their horses.

"Abby," Rebecca said, shaking her head a little. "That was beautiful! You and Beau took those jumps in perfect unison. Your timing was excellent, and I'm so happy with how you handled him. Well done!"

"Thank you so much!" I said, all smiles.

Everyone clapped. Although Selly was definitely fake-clapping, and I couldn't tell if Emery and Nina were too, but they probably were.

At this moment, I didn't care. I'd done my very best and so had Beau. There was nothing we could have done differently over those jumps. Sure, our flatwork had been a little rocky, but I couldn't change it now. I had to hope that what we'd done would be enough for Sasha and Heather to accept me into their winter clinic.

"Let's wrap it up for today," Rebecca said, her gaze going from one of us to the next. "I'm so proud of each of you. No matter what the results of your auditions, I want you to know that I'm thrilled you're putting yourselves out there." She gave us a lopsided smile. "Unfortunately, not everyone can be chosen. But all auditions are great experiences, and if you don't get into the winter clinic, there will be other opportunities."

But not with Sasha, I thought. She was so busy, and this clinic was one of the rare chances to work with her. I couldn't count on crossing my fingers that another opportunity to ride for her would happen, because I wasn't sure *if* or *when* it would ever come up.

"Thank you all for your hard work," Rebecca said. "Cool out your horses and take good care of them. Allie and I will have the footage from your rides up on the drive for everyone later tonight or tomorrow at the latest."

We nodded our thanks, and when Thea headed with Chaos to the cool-out lanes, I kept Beau in the arena. Mila had wandered away too, so I was on my own.

Have a Little Threat.
As a Treat!

LATER THAT EVENING, I WORKED ON MY homework in silence, ignoring most of Vivi's attempts at small talk. If I stopped being best friends with her now, it would hurt less when she and Thea inevitably dumped me.

After a while, Vivi gave up and left, mumbling some excuse about having somewhere she needed to be. But I knew her schedule. She didn't have anything tonight. Maybe she was even hanging out with Thea. Hurt made my eyes well up with tears.

So I focused on homework and got everything finished and put away for tomorrow. While I looked at my plants, I started my mental checklist of everything to do before the Halloween show. The list was long, but if I tackled some each week, I could handle it.

But there was one giant thing on my to-do list that I couldn't do on my own.

"Ugh, I have to text Nina," I told my plants. "I don't want to!"

But it needed to be done.

The sooner this was off my list, the better.

I sent her a quick text.

Abby: You free to meet and write that email to the IPL teams?

Much to my disappointment, she texted right back.

Nina: Yeah, Charles common room in ten?

Abby: Sure.

Charles House was where Nina and Emery lived, and while I wasn't excited to go there, I was very much ready to get this email behind us.

A few minutes later, I left my room with my laptop tucked under my arm and headed for Charles. Campus was fairly busy as students headed off to evening activities.

At Charles, I rang the doorbell, and when the door opened, a fuzzy-sock-clad Emery stood there, blinking at me.

"Um, hi," she said.

"I'm here for Nina," I said flatly.

"Oh." She moved out of the doorway so I could step inside. "Abby—"

I sighed, cutting her off. "Look, I'm not trying to be mean. But Emery, I still don't want to talk, okay? I'm here to write an email that I really, really wish I didn't have to write. I can't handle anything else right now."

"Okay, sorry," Emery whispered. She gave me a weak smile. "Good luck with the email."

Before she could try to talk to me again, I headed for the common room. Nina was cross-legged on the couch, scrolling on her phone. She saw me and grimaced.

"I don't want to do this," she said.

"Me either." I plopped down next to her on the sofa and opened my laptop. "But we have to. Or Rebecca will never let us off the hook."

"Why don't you write it and show me when you're done?"

I snorted. "Not a chance. We're doing this together or not at all."

"Fiiine." Nina folded her arms across her chest. "Let's get this over with."

I typed *Dear IPL teams*. Then I looked at Nina. "Now what?"

"Give me your laptop. This is going to take all night if you type."

Rolling my eyes, I handed her my laptop, and we spent the next half hour going back and forth on what to say and what to leave out before we settled on what seemed like a decent email.

> Dear IPL teams,
> We're the two riders who argued during the show we hosted at Foxbury. We'd like to apologize for our behavior. It was really selfish. We should have talked through our differences after the show, not during. Both of us are sorry for the disruption.
> We'd like to make it up to everyone with a pizza party at Foxbury for anyone who attended that show. It's on us!

Come over this Sunday at noon if you
want to eat and hang out.

Again, we're sorry.

Sincerely,

Nina Wilkerson and Abby St. Clair

Nina typed in the team's LISTSERV email address and let
the cursor hover over the send button.

"Ugh, once we send this, there's no taking it back," she said.

"But it's the truth. We *are* sorry."

"Yeah, but this apology will wind up on TikTok. You
know someone's gonna read it and make fun of us. Again."

I winced. "You're probably right."

Social media had not been kind to the "Foxbury Four," as
we'd been dubbed online, even though Thea had been trying
to stop the fight and Selly hadn't done anything. We'd been
labeled spoiled brats who couldn't wait until after the show to
argue. There were even comments from people who said they'd
seen Nina and me slap each other, which definitely had *not*
happened. Even if Nina had deserved it.

"All right, I'm sending it," Nina said.

She tapped send, and the email whooshed away.

"I feel a little sick," I said, taking my laptop back from her and closing the lid. "Apologizing was the right thing to do, I get it, but ugh, it doesn't feel great to think about facing everyone."

"Yeaaah. We can't hide from them forever, but seeing them is going to suck. I guess it's like ripping off a Band-Aid? At least we get it over with before we have to compete against them."

I nodded. "True. That would add an extra layer of stress to a comp."

"Now I'm going to be waiting for someone to tag us on socials and stir the whole mess up all over again."

"Or maybe no one will say anything, and this nightmare will die down." But even as I said it, I knew that wasn't going to happen. I glanced at my phone, wondering if I needed to turn off notifications for TikTok and Instagram for the next couple of days.

Nina settled back into the arm of the couch and looked at me sideways.

"What?" I asked hesitantly.

"Oh, nothing, really," she said, "except it's kind of funny that you're worried about people making fun of you."

I frowned. "So are you."

"But I don't have anything else to worry about. You, however . . ." Nina laughed. "You've got much bigger problems."

My stomach dropped. I tried to keep a neutral expression on my face, but I felt my entire body tense.

Nina caught my eye and smirked. "Clearly, I don't need to spell it out for you. You already know."

"Nina, you could talk to Selly," I said. "You could stop this before it blows up into something even bigger than it already is. We can't cause any trouble at the stable ever again or Rebecca will kick all of us out!"

"Please, do you think Selly would do anything to jeopardize her spot? She's way too smart for that."

"Hey, you and I didn't mean to get in a screaming match at the stable either, but it happened."

Nina rolled her eyes.

I wanted to plead with her to talk to her best friend and stop this, but I knew it wouldn't work. Thinking about what Selly was going to do made my stomach hurt.

I stood, clutching my laptop. "I should go. The only reason I came here was to write that email, and it's done now."

Nina nodded. "Yeah, go get some sleep. While you can. Although, I don't know how you'll be able to because when you close your eyes, all you'll be able to think about is when Selly's going to strike."

I'd heard enough. I started for the door.

"You know what I did to you?" Nina shook her head. "Selly's going to make that look like amateur hour. You won't know how, and you won't know when, but Selly is going to *destroy* you."

I couldn't get out of the room fast enough as Nina's words followed me all the way back to Amherst.

Is Mila In or Out?

O N SATURDAY, I GRABBED THE BUS TO Foxbury for Mila's riding team test. As I settled into my seat, Thea hurried onboard and took her usual seat next to me. It was a gray, overcast day, and it matched my mood.

"Hey," she said tentatively.

"Hi," I said.

We fell into silence. I tried not to think about how much I missed her, or I'd start crying.

"Long week, huh?" I finally asked.

"The longest."

I looked sideways at Thea. "I haven't seen you much. I mean, you're in class and riding, but we haven't talked."

Because you'd rather be with Vivi, I thought.

"Yeah, I know," she said. "Things are so busy right now."

"Right." I nodded, chewing on my bottom lip. "Busy for me, too."

I didn't ask her what she'd been busy doing, because I had a sinking feeling that the answer would hurt.

"Do you want to hang out tonight?" I asked. "We could order tons of food and watch a movie."

Thea glanced at her phone and then back at me. "I can't tonight."

"Oh."

I waited for her to tell me why and suggest another night for us to get together, but she didn't say anything, and we got off the bus without another word to each other.

I headed inside the stable while Thea went in the direction of the big arena. But I wished I'd gone the other way when Selly came out of Ember's stall. She latched the door and eyed me.

"Why are you here?" she asked. "To cheer on the baby riders?"

"Yup," I said. "It's called being a good teammate. You know, sportsmanship. That kinda thing."

Selly smirked. "Right. It's all fun and games until your little girlfriend makes our team."

I sighed. "That would be the worst. Another great rider joining us at lessons."

"Are you messing with me, or are you really that clueless?" Selly asked. She folded her arms across her chest. "With her on our team, she'll be another rider we—well, *you*—have to compete against to become a rising star."

Each spring, Rebecca hand-selected riders from any of her teams who showed extra promise. Those riders would work in intensive, more advanced sessions with her. My teammates and I had never been chosen. But I wanted to be picked more than anything next year. Those classes were what I needed to get me on track to becoming a career equestrian.

"Maybe we'll all get chosen," I said. "There's no rule that says we can't."

"Then it wouldn't be special, would it?" Selly snapped.

She was right. Unfortunately.

"Whatever," I said. "There's plenty of time to worry about that. We have enough going on."

"You're a pathetic excuse for a teammate," Selly said, her brown eyes flashing. "You better figure out how to be competitive and fast. I'm not going to let you sink our team because you want to play nice."

And with that, she stomped away.

I started down the aisle again, heading for Mila's horse Circe's stall. I'd been blowing Mila off, but I knew I had to say *something* to her before her test. I didn't want whatever was going on between us—or wasn't, at this point—to mess things up for her.

"Hey," I said, poking my head over the stall door.

Mila was inside, wrapping Circe's legs. She grinned when she saw me. "Hey! Where have you been? I've been texting you all week!"

"Sorry, I meant to text you back," I said. "I've just been . . . really busy."

Her face fell. "Oh. Gotcha."

"But I wanted to come and wish you good luck," I said. That made Mila smile.

"Thanks! I'm just getting Miss Thing ready."

Circe reached her muzzle in my direction and sniffed my hands.

"Nervous?" I asked.

"Terrified."

I wanted to reach out and squeeze Mila's hand. But I shoved my hands into my back pockets. "You're going to do great. Rebecca really believes in you."

I really believe in you.

Mila blushed, shifting from foot to foot. "Thank you. I'm so glad you're here."

I chewed on the inside of my cheek, forcing myself not to give her a giant, dumb smile. Instead, I nodded and said, "Of course. It's what teammates do."

"Yeah," Mila said after a long pause. "Teammates."

I left her to finish getting ready, and it wasn't long before she was mounted and in the arena.

Rebecca put her through the basics—walk, trot, canter, transitions, halts, circles, and serpentines. I squeezed the bench under me. I hadn't taken my eyes off Mila and Circe since they'd entered the arena, and as far as I could tell, the pair had been almost flawless.

"All right, ride over to me, please!" Rebecca called to Mila.

Mila trotted Circe over to Rebecca and brought the mare to a smooth stop in front of her.

"You're doing great," Rebecca said, "and you should be very proud. For the final part of the test, I'm going to ask you to warm up over a few jumps, then take those three obstacles over there." She pointed down at the other end of the arena. "Two verticals and an oxer. They're not any higher than what you're used to. Okay?"

I winced. Jumping made Mila nervous.

"Okay," Mila said, her voice clear. "You got it!"

I crossed my fingers on my right hand. And on my left. And tried to cross my toes, but that was impossible, so I curled them instead as I watched Mila warm up and then head for the minicourse.

"Go, Mila!" I cheered as she turned Circe in a circle.

A smile flashed on her face before she turned her back to us and headed down the arena. She made a half circle and lined Circe up with the jumps.

You can do this, you can do this, I chanted.

Mila was relaxed in the saddle as she urged Circe over the first vertical. The gray mare was knees to nose as she sailed over the jump and landed easily on the other side. Mila kept her at a steady canter toward the next set of red-and-white poles.

Three, two, one, now! I said to myself.

At precisely the right second, Mila lifted out of the saddle and pushed her hands up Circe's neck as the mare soared over the vertical with room to spare.

I stood in the stands, clasping my hands together in front of me. *C'mon, Mila!*

Mila and Circe reached the oxer, and my heart was in my throat while I watched. If Mila was nervous, she didn't show it. Her hands and legs were steady as she urged Circe over the oxer. The mare tucked her legs and jumped the spread with ease. She landed with a soft thud in the dirt.

"YES, Mila!" I yelled.

From down the bleachers, Thea clapped. "Way to go, Mila!"

Mila glanced at the stands, grinning, and pumped one of her fists in the air.

A smiling Rebecca waved her over to the center of the arena.

"Well, I can't even pretend to think about it," Rebecca said. "You'd be a wonderful asset to our middle novice team, Mila. You up for it?"

"Yes!" Mila said. "I'm *so* up for it!"

Rebecca nodded. "Great. Then we're thrilled to have you. You'll be riding with Abby, Keir, Emery, Selly, Thea, and Nina for lessons. How's that sound?"

"Perfect," Mila said. "Thank you so much."

"Thank *you* for your hard work. I'm excited to have you represent Foxbury. Go cool down Circe and get her turned out."

Mila nodded and turned Circe toward us. I climbed down from the bleachers, and Thea was a few steps behind me.

We went up to Mila and Circe, and I smiled at her.

"Congratulations!"

"I can't believe it!" Mila said, her cheeks flushed. She dismounted and loosened Circe's girth.

Thea waved her hand. "I can believe it. You're good! Welcome to our team!"

"Thank you! I'm so excited."

"Once you're done with Circe, how about we go get ice cream?" Thea asked, glancing at me. "We have to celebrate."

"I'd love that," Mila said.

"I—I can't," I said, backing away from them. No way was I going to get closer to Mila only to have her be hot and cold with me later like Thea and Vivi.

"Why?" Thea asked, knitting her brows together. "Do you have tons of homework or something?"

"I just can't, okay?" I said.

Thea folded her arms, glaring at me. "Fiiine." She turned to Mila. "Guess it's just us, then!"

I hated this! I wanted my best friends to be normal! And I wanted to get ice cream with Mila!

"I'm going to give Chaos a treat, but I'll come find you in a few," Thea told her. Then she headed off and left me standing very awkward and weird with Mila.

"Well, have fun with Thea!" I said, nonchalant and like I didn't care at *all* that I was missing this. "I better go."

"Abby! Wait," Mila said. She led Circe closer to me. So close, in fact, that I could smell Mila's fruity bubble gum. "I've been wanting to ask you something."

I swallowed hard, trying to keep a neutral expression on my face. "What's up?"

"I'm really excited about going to Salem with some people from school," Mila said.

Some of the area schools were driving students to Salem for a giant Halloween bash for epically scary fun.

"It'll be cool."

"Is there . . ." Mila looked down at her boots, a flush spreading across her cheeks. "Is there anyone you want to go to the party with?"

Oh. *Crap.*

She wasn't—was she? She could *not* be asking me out

right now! I didn't have the brain space to even handle going to the dance with anyone.

"Yeah," I blurted out.

Hope filled Mila's eyes. "Who?" She smiled at me, waiting for me to say her name. She had no idea how much I wanted to.

"This . . . girl from my science class," I lied, hating myself for every word. "I'm asking her."

Mila's hopeful expression crumpled right in front of my face. She tilted her head, trying to make sense of what I'd said. Then her eyes filled with tears. "Oh," she whispered. "I thought—never mind."

"See you," I managed to get out before turning away from her and dashing toward the bus. I started crying so hard, I couldn't even see.

Mila probably wouldn't talk to me ever again, and it felt *awful.*

Foxbury Four = United Front

LATER THE NEXT MORNING, I HOPPED on the bus so I could get to the stable early and start setting up for our pizza party. At least Mila wouldn't be at the stable today, and I wouldn't have to see how much I'd hurt her.

I groaned when Nina darted across the parking lot and hurried up the bus steps. She looked around, spotted me, and grinned.

Oh, *great*. I did not want to spend more time with her after our little chat the other day.

But Nina sauntered down the aisle and plopped into the seat next to me.

"Why?" I asked.

She laughed. "Because."

"Ninety-nine percent of the seats are free," I said. "You could sit literally anywhere. Still can!"

"But I wanted to sit with you," Nina said, pouting a little.

I sighed.

"Fiiine."

The bus ride was only a few minutes long, anyway. I could make it.

"So, I've noticed something," Nina said.

I steeled myself, because I knew whatever she said next was going to be rude or snarky.

"You've been alone a lot this week," she continued.

And there it was.

"No, I haven't," I lied.

"Um, yes, you have. Usually, you're with Thea or Vivi. But I've seen you alone in between classes, and you were by yourself at lunch yesterday."

I stared at my hands as I struggled not to pick at the already ragged cuticle on my thumb. "I'm not always with them. Plus, they're extra busy right now."

"Oh? With?"

"I don't know! Stuff!"

Nina shifted in her seat, turning her body toward me a little. She made me feel even more trapped against the window, with no easy way to get by her and into the aisle. "You don't know what your best friends are doing? Hmm, sounds suspicious to me."

"I—I meant . . ." I paused, taking a breath because she'd made me flustered. "I know what they're doing. I couldn't think of it on the spot. That's all."

Nina raised an eyebrow as she stared at me. "Mmmkay."

She didn't say anything else to me for the rest of the bus ride, but the damage had been done. I was rattled, and she knew it.

I sighed with relief when the bus stopped in the stable parking lot, and Nina got up. No more talking to her today, thank you.

We climbed off the bus and split up, and I headed for Beau's stall to say hi before going to find Rebecca.

Beau must have heard me coming, because I was steps away from his stall when he popped his head over the door and craned his neck in my direction.

"How are you, my handsome guy?" I asked him.

He let out a quiet *wuff* and sniffed my hands.

"You must be okay," I said, "because you're looking for a snack like always. Let's see here. . . ." I pretended to think. "Do I have any treats for Beau?"

He pointed both ears forward at the *T* word, and it made me laugh.

"Hmm. I'm not sure I do." I gave him an exaggerated shrug. "Do you even like treats?"

Beau leaned his chest against the stall door, extended his neck, and bumped my arm with his muzzle.

"Hey!" I laughed.

He bumped me again, a gleam in his eye. I'd teased him enough. I dug into my back pocket and found one of the peppermint hard candies I liked to give him from time to time. Like many horses, he loved, *loved* peppermint.

It took me a second to unwrap it because he kept reaching toward me and lipping the air.

"Wait," I told him, my voice firm.

He ducked his head a little and stopped pestering me.

"Good boy." I put the candy on my palm, flattened my fingers, and held out the treat to Beau.

He politely took the candy. While he crunched on it, I kissed his muzzle and told him I'd see him later. It was time to find Rebecca.

As I headed down the aisle, I smiled tentatively when I spotted a very familiar someone waving as she walked toward me.

"Hey!" Thea said. "Going to look for Rebecca?"

I nodded. "Yup. Want to walk with me?"

"Of course."

It crossed my mind to say something about how she'd ridden a different bus than me, but I held back. She seemed like her usual self.

"Today has already been so long," she said.

"I'm sorry." I frowned, looking at my best friend. "Everything . . . okay?"

She gave me a small smile. "I think it's my period. I got it this morning."

"Ugh, that would explain it. If you need Tylenol or Advil, I have some in my tack trunk."

"I took some before I got on the bus, but thanks, Abs."

We headed for Rebecca's office to talk to her before we got started with prep. Nina and Selly met up with us in the hallway, and we slowly shuffled inside.

"Nice to see you all," she said. "I'm sure you've been stressing over this party as much as I have."

"Most definitely," I said.

"It needs to go smoothly," Rebecca said, raising an eyebrow. "Got it?"

"Got it," Selly said. "We'll make this party perfect, Rebecca. Promise."

Thea, Nina, and I nodded. There was something in Selly's tone that sounded genuine and made me believe she was going to be a great hostess.

Rebecca softened. "Thank you. You'll find all the supplies in the main storage closet. Go get started on setting up and come talk to me if you need anything."

We left Rebecca's office, and in the hallway, Selly stopped and turned to the rest of us.

"I meant what I said in there," she said. "Let's work together to make this decent for everyone." She eyed me. "And then we can go back to hating each other. Cool?"

"Cool," I said.

Thea nodded. "Yup, I'm in. Should we have bought decorations?"

Selly snorted. "That say what? 'Congrats, we got in trouble, so here's pizza'?"

"Good point, I guess," Thea said. "Confetti would probably be a horrible idea too, then."

"Now I know you're trolling me," Selly said, rolling her eyes.

"I wasn't!" Thea protested. "I was trying to make this a good afternoon for everyone. Maybe if people have a fantastic time, they'll stop shading us on socials."

"No matter what we do, they'll post about it," Nina said. "I wish we could skip this stupid party."

I sighed. "Me too. But it's happening, so we have to make the best of it."

"You sound like a therapist," Selly said. "Can you not?"

I folded my arms across my chest and went quiet. There was enough going on today without arguing with Selly.

"Let's clean the meeting room first. Then set up cups and plates," Thea said.

And together, we wiped down the tables and swept the

floor. It didn't take long to get the room freshened up, and then Nina brought in an armful of plastic cups and paper plates. Selly got the napkins, and I hauled bottles of soda out of the fridge. We put out bowls of chips, Chex Mix, and M&M's. And before we knew it, it was nearly time for people to arrive.

"I have an idea," Selly said, "before everyone gets here."

Nina, Thea, and I looked at her.

"We should play offense," she said. "Let's film a TikTok and post it now. Like a 'Hey, this is the Foxbury Four, and we're throwing a party' and totally make everyone think we *want* to be doing this."

"That's a really good idea," Thea said.

I nodded. It was rare that I wanted to go along with anything Selly suggested, but this was one of those times. "Let's do it."

"Come stand by me," Selly said, motioning to us. She smoothed the sleeves of her oversized cream-colored sweater and twirled the ends of her ponytail. The girl always looked good with no primping necessary.

Thea, Nina, and I crowded around her, and she opened TikTok and held up her phone, angling it so we were all in the frame.

"Ready?" she asked.

"Ready," I said.

Nina and Thea nodded.

Selly tapped the record button, and we smiled for the camera.

"Hey, it's the Foxbury Four!" Selly said, charisma oozing out of her voice. "And we're hosting a pizza party!"

"If you were lucky enough to get an invite, we'll see you soon," Nina said.

"There's plenty of pizza for everyone," I added.

"Gotta go!" Thea said. "Guests are here!"

They weren't, but that sure sounded good.

"Byeee!" we said together.

Selly posted the video just as Rebecca called our names. "Your guests are arriving!" she said.

With one last look at each other, we slipped out of the meeting room and headed to greet them. It was time to put on a show of our own—one of a united front.

Still, I wanted to hide behind Thea when we joined Rebecca at the stable entrance and started welcoming in riders and ushering them into the meeting room.

"Thanks for coming," I said to Leo and Amir. They were

besties from another stable, and I liked hanging out with them.

"Anything for pizza," Leo said, flashing a grin.

Amir nodded. "Same."

Soon, almost all of the thirty people who had been invited were here. Riders scattered around the room, broken up into groups to talk and munch on snacks.

Rebecca walked over to Thea, Selly, Nina, and me. "I'm going to be in the conference room for a bit with the other instructors. But I'll order the pizzas and will bring them in when they get here, okay?"

"Okay," Selly said. "We got this."

We stuck together and moved around the room, talking to other riders. Some people were standoffish and not interested in talking, but others, like Leo and Amir, were fine with us and acted like they were over our fight.

"Pizza's here!" Rebecca said, walking into the room with a stack of delicious-smelling pizzas. The other instructors followed her, and I knew this was the moment we needed to apologize to everyone.

"Ready to do this?" I asked Nina, Selly, and Thea.

"Yup," Thea said. "Let's get it over with."

The four of us shuffled to the front of the room while Rebecca set the pizzas down on the folding table.

"Before we eat, we'd like to say something," I said, my voice shaking a little.

Everyone turned in our direction, and I tried not to let my knees go wobbly at all the pairs of eyes that were on us. Suddenly, it felt too warm and a little stuffy in here.

"We asked you here to have pizza, but we also wanted to apologize," Thea said.

It made me feel awful to see my best friend standing up here with me and apologizing for something she didn't even do. Selly, too. This had all been Nina and me.

"To be completely honest, Selly and Thea had nothing to do with this," I said. "It was my fault and Nina's. We should have talked after the show. We know that. I'm sorry we disrupted your rides."

"Abby's right," Nina said. Her hands shook a little as she clasped them together in front of her. "This is on us. I'm really sorry, and I hope you can forgive us."

"It'll never happen again," I said. Then I caught Rebecca's eye. "Promise. And we're sorry to Rebecca. It wasn't fair to her, either."

Rebecca gave me a soft smile.

"I'll agree to get over it if you give me first dibs on the pizza," Amir said.

"Me too!" Leo said, his eyes glued on the food.

The riders broke out in laughter.

"Deal," I said, giggling.

"Seriously, though, thanks for listening, and we hope you enjoy the food," Nina said. "Let's eat!"

And with that, the four of us exchanged relief-filled smiles and stepped away from the head of the room.

Now we'd done everything we could to make it up to the other riders and to Rebecca. It was time to move forward.

Last Tour Stop

WE CHOWED DOWN ON THE DELIcious pizza, and I devoured three slices of cheesy pepperoni without getting sauce or grease on my fave blue pullover. It was a win!

"So, this Canterwood show," Eliana said. She was a bubbly rider from Weston Stables. "I'm trying not to think about the fact that it's on Ava and Olivia's home turf."

"They'll never let us live it down if we don't do well," I said.

Selly rolled her eyes. "We'll beat them. They'll be quiet after that."

"We can't go all the way to Canterwood and lose," said Eliana.

"Or Ava and Olivia will brag about it for eternity," Amir said. "Nobody has time for that."

We all laughed, and as we kept talking about Canterwood, I settled back in my seat and felt like I could fall asleep. The anxiety-fueled adrenaline that I'd been dealing with because of this day was finally wearing off. I was so relieved this was over that I couldn't even process it.

Once everyone had finished their pizza, Rebecca stood up and motioned for silence.

"Thank you for coming," she said. "Before you head home, I wanted to say I'm proud of my riders. *All* of them."

That made me smile. At least one thing in my life wasn't a complete mess.

"I hope you know that going forward, Foxbury is a place you can depend on as a future host stable," Rebecca said. "And until then, we look forward to seeing you at Canterwood!"

With that, people started to say their goodbyes and head out. Once everyone was gone, and it was only the Foxbury Four left in the room, we let out a collective sigh of relief.

Selly caught my eye. "We're back to enemies now, St. Clair."

"I figured," I said flatly.

After I got back to Saddlehill, I tried to study, but all I could focus on was how very alone I was in my room, with Vivi out somewhere. I didn't want to bother her or Thea, but there was one person here I could talk to. One person who could *maybe* be a friend if I at least heard her out. Sighing, I pulled out my phone and typed a quick text.

Abby: Hey, are you around? I'd like to talk if you're free.

The response came immediately.

Emery: Of course! Courtyard in ten?

Abby: Perfect.

I started toward the courtyard before I could change my mind. I'd meant what I'd said to Emery that day at Charles House—that I couldn't handle figuring out things with her too, on top of my current issues with Thea and Vivi. But I'd realized, and I wasn't sure when it happened, that I needed to at least talk to Emery about the Nina mess. If I didn't, I was going to be the reason it kept dragging out.

All I wanted now was for things to move forward in a

better direction, especially since Emery wasn't going anywhere.

I got to the courtyard at the same time she did, and we traded awkward looks before sitting next to each other on a bench.

"Thanks for meeting me," I said.

Emery nodded, playing with the ends of her honey-blond hair. "I was surprised to hear from you."

I laughed a little. "I surprised myself, too. I wasn't exactly planning to text you today, but it kind of hit me after I left Foxbury that we needed to talk, or we'd be enemies forever." I took a breath. "And I have enough of those. I don't know what our relationship looks like right now because of everything that happened, but I wanted to at least hear you out and go from there."

"Thank you," Emery said, her tone soft. "I've been wanting to talk to you, obviously, and I tried hard not to keep bugging you. I know you weren't ready."

I drew my knees up to my chest and wrapped my arms around my legs. "I wasn't. But I'm here, and I'm listening."

Emery's smile was shaky, but she nodded. "When Nina told me you'd done something to Selly, and she was going to make you pay for it, I was so, so freaking naive." She shook her head. "I honestly thought she'd pull some silly, harmless prank on you. I didn't know her at all, and I swear, I had no idea that's what she meant."

"I believe you," I said.

Emery swallowed. "But the second I found out you were getting harassed with the blackmail, I knew it was Nina. I went to her and begged her to stop. She laughed at me and said if I told you . . . she'd target me next."

"What?" I shook my head. "I didn't know that, Emery. Oh my god."

"I didn't tell you, because I'd screwed up so bad. Even if Nina wasn't threatening me, I should have told you the second I found out what she was doing. I made the wrong decision, Abby, and I'm so sorry."

I sighed, feeling a rush of sympathy for my stepsister. "Yeah, but I get why you were scared. You're brand-new here. You didn't know Nina at all or what she was capable of."

"I knew I didn't have any dirt for her to use against me, but it also didn't seem to matter. Like, she'd invent stuff if it meant she could try to make my life miserable."

"Yup," I said. "For sure. That would have made me nervous too, to get on her bad side."

"But meanwhile, I watched as she kept tormenting you, and I was too scared to say anything." Emery's eyes filled with tears.

"Do I wish you would have told me?" I asked. "Obviously, yes. Do I also understand how terrifying and manipulative Nina is, and do I get why you were afraid of her? Also, yes."

"You don't have to say that," Emery said. "Trust me, I get it if you don't want to talk to me ever again after this."

"You could have texted me all of this, you know."

Emery looked down at her lap and then back at me. "No, it would have been just to clear my name. I'd done enough."

I was quiet for a moment. "I'm going through some things with my friends," I said finally. "And honestly, the thing I'm about to say to you is something Thea said to me, exactly: I wish you could have come to me so we could have figured this out together." I sighed. "Knowing all that I know now and everything I already knew about Nina, I understand why you didn't. But I think it would be good for us if you came to me if anything like this ever happens again."

Emery gave me a hopeful smile and bobbed her head. "I promise, Abby. I really, really hope it doesn't, but I swear that I'll talk to you if it does."

I could see all over her face how terrible she felt about the whole mess. And I didn't think she hated me or had wanted to be pulled into Nina's scheme. She'd been put in a tough position as a new kid here, and I had to hope that she'd learned from it.

I blew out a breath. "So. Can we kind of start over?"

"I'd really like that."

We smiled at each other. Genuine smiles, for the first time in a while.

"I'll see you at the stable for lessons tomorrow," I said, uncurling my legs and standing.

Emery hopped up from her spot on the bench. "Sounds good. We've got a show to practice for."

"We sure do."

With one more smile at each other, we turned and headed in opposite directions. I felt lighter than I had in a long, long time. One crisis was handled.

When I got back in my room and settled on my bed, I pulled a knitted blanket over my lap and FaceTimed Dad. It had been a few days, and I didn't want him to worry.

"Hey, sweetie!" he answered.

"Hi, Dad!"

Just seeing his face helped a little. He was familiar, and seeing him was like having a piece of home here with me.

"How's my girl?" he asked.

"Not bad," I said. "Busy. But about to be even busier!"

Dad looked at me sideways. "Oh yeah? How come?"

I explained to him all about Sasha's clinic and the Halloween show at Canterwood. I told him how much I wanted to get into the clinic, but I explained that even if he let me apply, I'd still have to be chosen from all the applicants to attend. Thankfully, he said of course I could apply, since it meant so much. And he listened to me go on and on for about ten solid minutes about the Canterwood show and how ridiculously excited I was to set foot on that campus.

"So, what you're saying is that you're doing super well and have a lot to look forward to?" Dad asked, smiling at me.

"Yup. There's a lot of work to do before the show, but I'll get it done."

As we talked and he told me what was going on at home, my mind wandered to the show. I always rode with Thea and shared a room with her. Would I have to room with Selly or Nina? Barf.

"Abby?" Dad's voice cut through my worry.

"Sorry, yeah, the new shrimp recipe sounds great, Dad. I can't wait to try it when I'm home."

That made him smile. Whew.

"How are Thea and Vivi?" Dad asked. "I half expected Vivi to be on our FaceTime too, since you're always together."

Yeah, not anymore.

"They're good," I said slowly. "Vivi's with her other friends right now. Thea's"—I had no idea where Thea was or what she was doing—"probably out with her friends."

"Good, hon. Well, I'm sorry I can't make it to the Canterwood show to watch you and Emery ride, but I'm sure I'll see a video of it. And you know I'll be at the next one that's closer to home. I promise."

"I know, Dad. And it's totally okay that you're not coming to Canterwood."

I knew he couldn't take all that time off work to travel to Connecticut for a show, and I wouldn't expect him to do that.

We talked for a few more minutes before saying our good-byes, and when I hung up, I was wiped. Pretending everything was fine was harder than it sounded.

I opened Instagram, wanting to zone out for a few, and scrolled past a photo of Thea and Vivi—wait.

What?

Frantically, I scrolled back up. Cora, Thea's younger sister, had posted a pic of her, Vivi, and Thea. Cora sat between my two best friends, smiling. They were seated in the school theater, up near the stage, from the looks of it.

My best friends and my best friend's sister were hanging out without me.

Tears blurred my vision as I stared at the photo. The caption's words swam in front of me as I struggled to read it. *Best night in a while!*

Thea and Vivi hadn't said a word about going out with Cora.

Were they *mad* at me?

Hello, Ghostie

THE NEXT WEEK PASSED IN A BLUR OF riding and classes. On Friday, I studied alone in the library after classes, grabbed dinner at the caf, and then headed to my room to chill.

The sky was gray with thick clouds, and a light breeze kicked up dead leaves that skittered in front of me. Most of the buildings had pumpkins near the entrances, and looking at them made me sad. Halloween was one of my favorite times of the year, and I couldn't fully enjoy it because I wasn't really spending time with Vivi and Thea.

And I'd crushed Mila so hard that she hadn't looked at me once this week. Rebecca had put her on my competition team, though, so we'd have to start talking at the Canterwood show if we weren't before.

I let myself into Amherst and went straight to my room. Vivi looked up from where she stood near the fireplace and smiled.

"Hey," she said.

"Hi."

My eye caught on the orange fairy lights she'd turned on. There was a bowl of popcorn on Vivi's desk, and she'd arranged a bunch of pillows in a circle on the floor.

"What's going on?" I asked, putting down my backpack.

Vivi gave me a sheepish smile. "I thought it would be fun to play with Thea's Ouija board tonight and watch a scary movie. She wants to read tarot cards too."

"Oh."

I don't know why I was surprised. They'd been hanging out a lot without me. So why would tonight be any different?

"I would have asked you," Vivi said, "but you're, like, never around."

Because you're *always busy with Thea!* But I didn't want to fight with her, so I kept that to myself.

I waved my hand. "No big deal." Even though it was. And I kept saying everything was NBD to Thea and Vivi when that couldn't have been further from the truth. "I can go hang in the common room or something. I don't want to crash."

"Abby, seriously? *Stay!*" Vivi said. She gave me a look like I was ridiculous for even suggesting it. "It'll be fun!"

I'd missed her and Thea so much over the past couple of weeks. All I'd wanted was to hang out with them and have things go back to normal.

"Well, if you're sure," I said.

"Of course I am!" Vivi said, smiling. "And guess what?"

I eyed her, feeling better than I had in weeks. "Hmm?"

"Mila's coming!"

And just like that, my good mood evaporated.

"What?" I asked, horrified. This was the *worst* idea!

"Thea invited her," Vivi said. She fluttered around, turning on flameless candles and hitting play on a spooky lo-fi Spotify playlist. "It'll be *great*!"

"Yeah," I said weakly. "Great."

"They'll be here soon!" Vivi said. "I'm going to run down-stairs and grab snacks."

After she breezed out of the room, I scrubbed my face with my hands. *Ugh*. I wanted to bail, but that would make Mila feel worse. She'd probably think I didn't even want to be around her at all. Plus, with the Canterwood show coming up, we were going to be forced to spend time together. So maybe this was a good idea. We'd have to talk and not avoid each other.

I didn't have much time to stress, because it wasn't long before Mila and Thea arrived.

I tried to smile at Mila, but I could feel the awkward gri-mace on my face instead. "Hi," I said.

"Hey." She barely looked at me before sitting next to Thea.

We sat in a circle on the floor and stared at Thea's Ouija board. We'd decided to play with the board and then do tarot cards, saving the movie for last. Despite feeling like I was on edge with everyone, I was determined to have one normal night. Maybe it would help Thea and Vivi remember that I was their best friend too, and they wouldn't want to exclude me anymore.

"Should we be scared of it?" I asked. "The board, I mean."

The four of us looked at each other.

"I . . . hope not," Mila said.

"Have you used it before?" I asked Thea. "Basically, have you been haunted, is what I'm asking."

Thea laughed. "Yes, I've used it before. No, I have not been haunted."

I side-eyed her. "I'm trusting you here."

"So, what do we ask it?" Vivi asked, taking a bite of a Twizzler.

"Anything we want!" Thea said. "But let's start with something easy."

We leaned forward and put our fingers on the planchette. I'd played with a board a few times and knew that we had to ask yes-or-no questions, and the spirits would help us guide the planchette around to their desired answers.

"Hello," Thea said. "I'm Thea, and these are my friends. Is there anyone here?"

We waited, watching the board, and I almost couldn't believe it as the planchette moved to *YES*. Everyone gasped!

"Are you—" Mila started.

"—moving it?" I finished.

"No!" Vivi said. "Are you?"

The rest of us shook our heads.

"It moved on its own," I whispered.

"Are you a mean ghost?" Vivi asked the board.

The planchette moved to *NO*.

"Oh, whew," Vivi said.

"I feel better now about asking them questions," I said.

Mila nodded. "Me too." She cleared her throat. "Did you attend this school?"

The planchette went straight to *YES*.

"Oh my god!" I said. "Were you a student?"

Back to *YES*.

"Wow, hi!" Thea said. "Uh, thanks for hanging out with us! It's cool to, erm, meet another student."

We asked a few more questions, but the ghost must have floated to someone else's room after that question, because they didn't respond anymore. But it had been a good icebreaker.

"Let's put the board away," I said, shivering.

"I'm glad we're stopping before we run into a mean ghost," Vivi said. "But how cool that we communicated with a Saddlehill ghost!"

"Maybe they'll tell us their name next time," Thea said. "I bet they got shy."

"Come back and visit us, ghostie!" Vivi said. "When we have the lights on and we're trying to talk, of course. Not, like, randomly when we're sleeping. Thank you."

We giggled.

"Are we ready for tarot readings?" Thea asked, wiggling her eyebrows. "Because I'm so excited to do them!"

"I am," I said, unwrapping a banana-flavored Laffy Taffy.

"And me!" Mila said.

Vivi nodded. "You know I am."

"Excellent," Thea said.

She leaned over and grabbed her tarot deck from her bag. She took a moment to shuffle the cards.

"I've never done this before," Mila said, smiling at Thea. "This is gonna be fun!"

"Let me shuffle one more time," Thea said. "And then I'll pull a card for Mila. She can go first, since she's our newest friend."

Once Thea finished, she put the stack of cards on the carpet and waved her hands over them. Then she plucked the top card from the deck, turned it over, and placed it faceup next to the deck.

"Ooh," Thea said, smiling. "That's a *great* card, Mila! You got the Magician upright!"

We peered at the card, looking at the man pointing one hand up toward the universe and the other down to earth.

"What does it mean?" Mila asked. "He looks cool!"

"So, since we got him 'upright' in the deck, it means good things," Thea said. "This card is about your resourcefulness and power. You have a new beginning and lots of good opportunities coming." Thea smiled at Mila. "It also says you've got everything you need to succeed, and you have unlimited potential. All you have to do is tap into it!"

"That's *awesome*," Mila said. She puffed up her chest a little. "Wow, I feel really powerful!"

Was the card talking about her new beginning . . . away from me?

"Abby next!" Vivi said.

Thea nodded and picked up the deck. "Let me reshuffle with Abby in mind."

The three of us munched on candy while we waited for the cards to be just right for Thea.

"The cards feel ready," Thea said. She put them down, hand hovering over the deck. "Give me the right card for Abby, please."

I loved watching Thea do this. She took it seriously and

treated it like an art form, which it kind of was. She was always reading more about the cards, and heck, she'd memorized all of them and what they meant. I wasn't sure how many cards there were exactly, but it seemed like a lot. Definitely more than fifty.

Thea turned over a card and winced.

"Nooo," I said. "Not a bad card!"

"Is it bad?" Mila asked Thea, eyes wide.

"It's not . . . *great*," Thea said. "But remember! They're just cards. They might not even mean anything."

"What is it, and what does it mean?" I grumbled.

"It's the Five of Wands upright," Thea said. "It means tension and conflict. And competition."

"So, this card is about the Canterwood show," I said.

I stared at the card, which had five men fighting each other with wands raised.

"The Five of Wands typically means there's distrust among people," Thea said. "It means people can't get along, and they fight."

"Oh." I sighed. "Maybe it was more about me and Selly and less about Canterwood."

"Maybe," Thea said.

The more I thought about it, the less idea I had of what

the card was talking about. My life had a lot of conflict and distrust at the moment. Looking around at the other people in this room, the card could have been about any one of them.

And that was scarier than any possibly haunted Ouija board.

Oohs & Oddities

THE NEXT WEEK WENT SLIGHTLY better than the week before it. At lessons, Mila and I managed to make small talk, even if it was awkward. Vivi, Thea, and I had sort of started to fall back into our old friendship patterns. But they were still busy a lot, leaving me on my own.

When Saturday rolled around, I was practically bouncing off the walls. It was Salem day, and I was determined to have the best time. Plus, it was the *perfect* opportunity for me to hang out with Thea and Vivi. Maybe they'd remember what a great bestie I was and stop ignoring me so much.

Today was going to be a happily haunted day.

No friendship weirdness.

No awkwardness with Mila.

No arguments with Selly and Nina.

Just fun in Salem, no matter what. Thankfully, Vivi seemed to be on the same page, because she'd been chatty all day. For a second, I'd wanted to ask her about her time out with Cora and Thea, but I'd vowed not to ruin this day, so I'd kept my mouth shut.

"Is it time to go yet?" I asked Vivi for the hundredth time.

She looked up from her desk chair, where she'd sat to apply some Halloween party makeup.

Vivi checked her phone. "Five minutes!"

"I'm going to *die*," I said dramatically. Who knew it would take one o'clock so long to get here? "I'm ready to go now!"

Molly and several other resident advisors were tagging along with the adults as chaperones, and teachers from Mila's school were coming too, to accompany their students.

I stood in front of our full-length mirror and checked my outfit again. I'd gone with a flared black sweaterdress with a gold-striped skirt. Molly had stopped by this morning to remind us to wear boots or comfortable shoes with our outfits, since there was a lot to see in Salem, and we had plans to explore before going to the party.

"I'm ready!" Vivi said, grinning at me. She'd applied glitter to her cheeks and eyelids, and she looked supercute in flowy black pants and a bloodred sweater. She picked up a devil-horns headband and slid it on.

"We look so cute with our headbands!" I said, adjusting my cat ears.

"Selfie?" Vivi asked.

The fact that she asked instead of just coming over and taking it with me was weird. But I brushed it off, determined not to let it worry me more about the state of our friendship.

We mushed our faces together and smiled at the camera. Then we headed downstairs to find Molly. She came into the living room and smiled at us.

"Ready to go?" she asked.

We all nodded as Selly came down from upstairs and joined us. She had on a fuzzy white sweater, black pants, and an angel-halo headband.

Oh, the irony.

"So ready!" I said.

We headed out to the parking lot, where Thea, Emery, and a bunch of other people I recognized from classes were waiting.

The adults split us up into the waiting fleet of SUVs, and the trip was *on*!

When we rolled into Salem less than an hour later, it was *packed*. It felt like being at Disney World!

"I didn't think it would be *this* busy!" I said. "I mean, I get it, but daaang."

Vivi shook her head. "Do we still get to explore?" she asked Molly.

"Yes, but in groups," Molly said. "No one's heading off on their own because of the crowds. But the ballroom we rented with the other area schools is private, so that will be much quieter."

That helped a little. There were tourists everywhere, and a lot of them were in Halloween costumes. It was kind of overwhelming to see so many costumed people in one space. But there were tons of families and lots of kids, so it wasn't too intimidating.

We'd decided not to do any official tourist activities like the trolley guided tour or get tickets to the Salem Witch

Museum. Instead, we'd planned to walk around and check out the Salem Haunted Happenings festival.

We climbed out of the SUV, and I huddled up with my friends, joining Willa and Ankita, who had ridden in the other SUV. And Selly and Nina.

My phone chimed, and I glanced at the screen.

Mila had group texted me, Thea, and Vivi.

Mila: Here! Looking for you!

I texted her back and told her where our group was, and seconds later, I spotted Mila and one of her teachers heading in our direction.

Mila looked painfully cute. She'd paired a dark purple skirt and dark tights with spiders all over them with a chunky black sweater that had tiny skulls on the sleeves. I wanted to tell her how much I loved her outfit, but I smiled and said hi instead.

Mila's teacher introduced herself to Molly, and my RA promised she'd keep an eye on Mila, since she had permission to hang with our group today.

"Let's quickly talk about the plan," Molly said. "If all nine of you stick together, and by 'together,' I mean within reach of each other, you may check out the festival. I'll be walking around with the other RAs too, so I'll be right there."

"Sounds good!" I said.

"If you're anxious or don't think your group wants to stay together," Molly said, "you can also hang out with me or any of the other resident advisors."

"We'll be a group," Emery said, and everyone else chimed in that we would.

"Great," Molly said. "Let's meet in front of the Salem Witch Museum in an hour and a half. Then we'll head to the ballroom to party!"

"I'll set an alarm," Willa said, "so we'll be there on time!"

Molly smiled. "Perfect. Have fun!"

She stepped away from our group to talk to the other RAs, and everyone smiled at each other. We'd been turned loose! Things weren't great between Mila and me, but I had to hope that being in a group of friends would keep the worst of the awkwardness away.

"I've got my guide!" Thea said, holding up a thick stack of papers. "I printed it when I knew we were coming."

"Dork," Selly said. "And what are you, my grandma? She refuses to use anything but paper maps and directions when she has, you know, a *phone*."

"You don't have to use my guide," Thea said sweetly.

But Selly edged closer to Thea as she flipped through the pages and told us what was going on and where.

"There are fortune-tellers, haunted houses, live music, a costume parade . . . basically, anything creepy you can think of, this place has it," Thea said.

"We all have to agree on what we do," I said. "Or we're back with Molly."

"And I don't want to waste time arguing," Vivi said, with a quick glance at Nina and Selly. "So let's vote and decide."

"There's really only one thing I want to do more than anything while I'm here," Selly said. "And that's go to a haunted house."

"Me too!" Emery said.

Ankita nodded. "I do too. Even if Willa has to hold my hand."

The rest of us traded looks.

"I'm in," I said. "That's kind of the whole point of Salem, right? To get scared?"

Quickly, Thea flipped to the section on haunted houses in her guidebook. "There are, like, *five* haunted houses," she said. "See? There's Chambers of Terror, Frankenstein's Castle, Haunted Witch Village."

"Witch Mansion Haunted House," Willa read over her shoulder. "And the Lost Museum at Gallows Hill."

We read the descriptions and scare factors for each one.

"I'll say it," Vivi said. "I think Chambers of Terror is too much for me."

"Baby," Nina said.

But relief flashed on Selly's face. "Agreed," she said quickly. "I mean, yeah, I think it's too intense for the rest of you."

"Ooh, how about this one?" I tapped the paper, pointing to Oohs & Oddities Haunted House. "It just opened this year!"

I held my breath, expecting Selly and Nina to argue. But they nodded. And so did everyone else.

Thea navigated while using her guide, and we found the haunted house easily.

"The line's short!" Ankita cheered. "Good choice!"

"Maybe the long line is for the Chambers of Terror," I said, shivering. "No, thank you."

We reached the ticket booth, and a very tall witch exchanged our money for tickets. Suddenly, this seemed like the *wrong* choice of activity today. I'd never been in a haunted house, and while I had a feeling I knew what went on in one, I also wasn't sure what to expect. I swallowed hard and looked over at Mila. She seemed cool and calm, so I followed her through the entrance. Thea was on my heels, and the rest of our group was right behind us.

We walked into the dark house, lit only by bare light bulbs and the occasional lamp with a flickering bulb in it.

There was a giant oil painting of the home's first owners at the entryway. I stepped closer to peer at it and jumped back when the people blinked!

"Oh my god!" I said to Mila. "Did you see that?!"

"What?" she asked, peering at it.

They blinked again, and laughing, we hurried away from the painting and into the living room.

"This is *so* not like watching a scary movie!" I said. "It's fine when I'm in my own environment and not standing in a haunted house with creepy things waiting to get me!"

"Do you want to go?" Mila asked. "We can bail and wait for everyone right outside."

I shook my head. "No. Well, not yet, anyway. It's kind of fun being scared. It's just *very* different."

"If it stops being fun for anyone, we can leave," Thea said.

"Definitely," I said.

We wound our way through the haunted house, laughing

and screaming at the ghouls, goblins, and masked figures that popped out of mirrors, jumped at us from around corners, and hid behind every door.

The poorly lit areas added to the creep factor, and I had to keep looking twice to see if something was a shadow or a monster. One of the upstairs rooms had a terrifying room filled with old porcelain dolls with cracked faces.

"If one of these dolls starts talking, I'm *out of here*," Mila whispered.

Breathlessly, I nodded.

The bedroom door slammed shut behind us, and Mila shrieked.

"C'mon!" I said, unable to stop myself from grabbing her hand and tugging. We yanked open the door, and there was no one on the other side. We hurried down the hallway, almost colliding with the rest of our group.

"There's an evil clown that way!" Selly said. Even in the dim light, I could see her flushed cheeks. "Go the other way!"

As a group, we clustered together and made a run for it. We dashed for the exit, tumbling out of the house together, and nearly tripped on each other as we hit the pavement outside.

"Oh my god!" Nina said, her eyes wide. "That was wild!"

Everyone started talking at once.

"Did you see the ghost in the bathroom mirror?" Selly asked.

"I *hated* the clown!" Thea said.

"The doll room!" Mila added, shivering. "That's a whole lot of nope!"

"The bones in the fireplace? I swear, they moved!" said Ankita.

We all started laughing.

"I need something sweet and happy now," I said, putting a hand over my heart.

"Parade?" Thea asked.

"Please," I said.

And without a single argument, my group practically clung to each other as we walked away from the house and headed back down the street.

Sisterly Shoulder
to Cry On

MY FRIENDS AND I HUNG OUT AND
watched the parade for a while and enjoyed all
the costumes.

"Look," Thea said. "There's a Dalmatian in a suit! He even has a little monocle!"

There were so many costumed people—and pets!—in the parade. It was magical! People on floats threw out candy, and I scrambled to pick up some pieces, like I didn't have bowls of it at home.

Everyone was having a great time, and the anxiety I'd had

earlier about being in the crowded streets had faded. Being among friends had helped, and I'd gotten used to being around all the people.

Way too soon, it was time to meet Molly in front of the museum, so we headed off to find her.

"That was so fun," Willa said, unwrapping a Tootsie Roll. "I have the best costume ideas for next year after seeing some of those!"

"I want a Halloween parade on horseback," I said. "It would be epic!"

Selly caught my eye and nodded slowly. "That's actually a really good idea," she said. "You should talk to Rebecca about that."

"Maybe I will," I said.

We found Molly and the other RAs standing in front of the museum.

"Did you have fun?" Molly asked.

I smiled. "Aside from being nearly scared to death, yeah, I think we had fun."

"I'm good on haunted houses for a while," Ankita said. "Once might have been enough for me!"

We told Molly all about it as we walked to a nearby brick

building. Inside, Molly talked to a couple of people, who instructed us to follow the signs to our reserved ballroom.

And when we went down the hallway and pushed open the door, I was not the only person to gasp.

"Salem does *not* disappoint!" I said. "Wow!"

My eyes didn't know where to look first. The darkened room was lit by exquisite black chandeliers draped in black beads. Red spotlights were trained on a small stage for the band that was coming to play. There was a balcony in the back that was draped in deep purple silk fabric, and everything about this place screamed paranormal ball.

"This is pretty great," Selly said, taking it all in.

Banquet tables with fruit punch, finger food, and snacks were all set up under one of the windows. The shiny wooden floors gleamed, and I could not wait to get out there and dance! While we checked out the rest of the room, more students from Saddlehill and some who were from Mila's school came in.

Speakers crackled on, and someone hit play on a creepy playlist. "This Is Halloween" from *The Nightmare Before Christmas* started playing, and I cheered. "Let's go!"

A few moments later, a local band took the stage and played some songs from the playlist.

My friends and I started dancing, and we lost ourselves in the music. When "Grim Grinning Ghosts" came on, we scream-sang the lyrics, and when "Monster Mash" played, Ankita and I did an entire freaking *routine* to it.

As the band covered another Halloween bop, a net at the top of the ballroom ceiling opened, and hundreds of red and black balloons floated down. We batted them through the air, trying to keep them from touching the floor until we were out of breath from laughing so hard and chasing the balloons.

"Let's get closer to the stage!" Ankita said. She pulled Willa forward with her.

Emery came over to me, smiling. "Hey," she said. "This is pretty wild!"

"I know, right? We're partying in Salem. Who gets to do that?!"

Emery nodded. "Exactly!"

We watched people dance and sipped our drinks. I realized how comfortable I felt around Emery now, and it felt *good* to spend time with her.

"So, you've been here a little while now," I said. "Are you glad you came to Saddlehill? And Foxbury?"

Emery glanced at me. "Honestly, I'm glad I *stayed*. When everything was going down with Nina, I thought about going home."

"You did?" I blinked, shaking my head. "I'm sorry."

"Yeah. I felt like I'd ruined your life by not coming forward. And I was scared that Nina was going to come after me next. So, I spent a lot of time thinking about calling my mom and saying I needed to leave."

Hearing that crushed me a little. "I hate that Nina almost wrecked everything for you."

Emery gave me a sad smile. "Yeah. I'd been so excited to come to Saddlehill and get to know you better. Like, it was all I thought about for weeks before we came."

I looked at her, taking this all in. "I really didn't know that you wanted to spend time with me. I thought you felt weird about our parents getting married and us becoming this, like, insta-fam. So I left you alone."

Emery shook her head. "No! But that's why I kind of ignored you, too. I didn't want to bother you. Now that I'm thinking about it, of course, it would look like I didn't want to get to know you."

We sighed simultaneously. Then giggled.

"We both messed up," I said. "But now we can work toward becoming friends."

"Yeah," Emery said, smiling. "Friends would be great."

I glanced across the dance floor and spotted Mila talking to a pretty girl with short blond hair that I'd seen hanging out with the group of kids from Mila's school.

The girl leaned in to talk to Mila, and whatever she said made Mila nod. And Mila smiled at her with that *look* she'd given me on the day we'd met. The look that had made me melt. A look I'd thought was just for me.

Then, together, they moved to an empty space on the dance floor.

All the surrounding noise fell away, and my heartbeat thudded in my ears as I watched them.

The blonde put her hands on Mila's waist, and Mila put her hands on the girl's shoulders. They giggled, and before I could watch another second, I turned away, tears filling my eyes.

"Abby?" Emery asked. "Are you okay?"

I couldn't talk about this. Not tonight. If I said one word, I'd break down.

"I'm fine," I croaked. But I wasn't. At all. Seeing Mila

with another girl was the *worst*. It felt like I'd been punched in the gut.

Emery touched my arm. "Why don't we get some fresh air?"

I nodded, and through a blur of tears, I followed Emery out into an empty hallway.

"I can't believe Mila would do that," Emery said, clenching her jaw. "I thought she liked you!"

"It's not her fault," I said. "It's mine."

Emery pursed her lips. "Abby, you don't have to protect her. I know you like her, but that was an awful thing to do."

"I'm not protecting her," I said. "She's dancing with that girl because I told her I was asking someone else to the dance."

"You did *what*?" Emery's eyes widened. "Why? Don't you like Mila?"

"Yes." I tried not to start crying. "I like her a lot."

Emery looked confused. "Okay, so then what's the problem? If you like Mila, you need to tell her!"

I shook my head. "I can't." I hadn't planned on telling Emery any of this, but it spilled out of me before I could stop it. "My own best friends are ignoring me most of the time. Clearly, there's something wrong with me. And Mila?" Tears pricked my eyes. "Mila's *amazing*. I didn't even have time to text her back because I was too freaked out about my best friends hating me! And then things got all messy and weird!"

"Abby." Emery put her hands on my shoulders. "It happens. Explain to her and tell her what's going on."

I groaned.

"And if something's going on with Vivi and Thea, you need to talk to them. *Communicate.*"

I wrinkled my nose. "*No.* Then they'd tell me what I don't want to hear! That they're best friends, and they don't want to be mine anymore."

Emery put her hands down by her sides and shrugged. "Then we deal with that. But I don't think that's it. Like, at all."

"They're always together," I said. *"Always."*

"Okay, maybe they're both going through something you don't know about. Or maybe they don't want to bug you. Or maybe they know you're extra busy right now, and they naturally got tighter."

"But I introduced them," I said. "And now they're ditching me!"

"Then *tell* them. You have to. Otherwise? You're going to keep thinking it's your fault, and then you'll ruin things with the girl you really like, and you'll have to watch her dance with another girl!"

I groaned again. "This is a disaster."

"Kinda," Emery said. "But it's fixable. I think, anyway."

"Maybe with Thea and Vivi," I said, "but Mila's moved on. I can't mess that up."

Emery shook her head. "I guess we'll tackle one crisis at a time. Thea and Vivi first. You need to hear it from them that you aren't an awful friend, and then you can go to Mila."

I gave her a tiny smile, and as much as I didn't want to talk to Thea and Vivi about this, I knew I had to. Soon.

Friends, Right?

I'D TRIED AND FAILED ALL OF SUNDAY TO talk to Vivi and Thea. Every time I opened my mouth to ask Vivi if she could talk, I clammed up.

After school on Monday, I headed to the stable and tacked up as dread pooled in my stomach.

Today would be the first time I'd see Mila since the dance in Salem. After Emery had given me the hallway pep talk, we'd gone back into the ballroom, and Mila and her mystery girl danced to a few more songs before the night was over. No one but Emery had noticed that I was upset, and I'd worked hard to stay away from Mila so she couldn't see that it bothered me so much.

I was the first rider in the big outdoor arena, and slowly, I let Beau amble along the rail as we started our warm-up. There were ground poles set up with some jumps, and I hoped they were for us!

Mila and Circe came into the arena, and Mila kept her mare at the opposite end of the arena.

Beau stretched his neck as we walked, and I leaned forward and patted his shoulder. "We're going to do great today, boy."

Beau bobbed his head and snorted like he agreed with me.

I glanced up as Selly, Nina, and Thea rode their horses into the arena. Selly pointed her dark bay mare, Ember, right at Mila and Circe. Nina and her gray gelding, Adore, were on Selly and Ember's heels.

"Hey, Mila," Selly said.

"Hi," Mila said, her tone unsure. I'd told her some of the horrible things Selly had done to me, so she wasn't eager to share the arena with Selly. Or Nina, for that matter.

"Look, I take this team seriously," Selly said. "Very seriously. The Canterwood show is important, and I want to secure more points toward becoming this year's junior champion rider."

Mila halted Circe and stared at Selly. "I'm confused. What made you think I don't take riding seriously? I got to practice before you, right?"

Selly's pretty face flushed. "I—yes, you did, but only because I was making sure Ember's tack was spotless." She narrowed her eyes. "Your saddle pad has a stain."

Mila shrugged. "I think we'll make it through practice in our lesson saddle pad just fine. But thanks for reminding me to get it in the wash!"

"Listen," Selly snapped. "I'm not messing around. I don't know what's going on between you and St. Clair, but I don't want it—"

"Nothing is going on," Mila said, her tone flat. "We're friends, right, Abby?"

That made me swallow. Hard. But Mila was right. Thanks to me, nothing was going on between us.

"Yeah. Friends," I said.

Selly stared Mila down. "Well, I want to win this year, and practices are important. So you better come prepared and not let anything—or *anyone*—get in the way."

"I stay prepared," Mila said.

Selly wilted in the saddle before straightening up and

pushing her shoulders back. "I guess we'll see, won't we?" she asked coolly.

Mila nodded, then cued Circe away from a very disgruntled Selly. I nudged Beau forward and got him moving at a brisk trot to keep Selly from coming over and going off on me next.

But before she could even think about saying anything else, Rebecca strode into the arena and stopped in the center. She waved us over, and we lined up our horses in front of her. Keir and Emery were with us, and I'd been so engrossed in the Selly-versus-Mila moment that I hadn't even noticed them and their horses joining us.

"Happy Monday, everyone," Rebecca said, smiling. "It's good to see you all!"

We nodded back.

Rebecca looked extra no-nonsense today, with her long brown hair up in a bun and a hand planted on her hip. "Let's get to our lesson, shall we? Today you're going to ask your horses to pay attention to every step they make and where they place their feet. So, look at the gymnastic course I set up."

I tried to shake off the Selly-and-Mila conversation. Today's lesson was going to take all my concentration.

"We're going to be working on balance," Rebecca said. "I

want to see your horse moving in a straight line. We'll start with low jumps for the first couple of rounds, and then I'll add some height. Okay?"

"Got it," I said along with my teammates.

"Mila, let's see you and Circe go first," Rebecca said. "Begin at a medium trot and then pick up a canter after the first cross rail."

Mila nodded and let Circe walk a beat before asking her to trot. The gray mare's tail streamed behind her as she trotted over the first three ground poles and hopped over the cross rail. She bounced perfectly through the rest of the course, and when she got to the last obstacle—a vertical—she increased her speed too much and jumped before Mila was ready. Because the rail was so low, they made it over without a problem. But when Mila turned back to face the group, she shook her head.

"That last one got us!" she said. "I wanted to keep her steady the whole time, but she got excited at the end."

"You'll do better on the next round," Rebecca said. "Keir, your turn."

I watched the rest of my teammates while I waited for my ride. Everyone was on fire today, and the horses had an extra spring in their steps, as if they knew we were in go mode. Every practice before the weekend show at Canterwood was important.

"Abby, you're up!" Rebecca said. "I want to see Beau start at a relaxed trot."

I nodded. Beau and I could do this! Eight ground poles, two cross rails, and one vertical at the end.

I squeezed my legs against Beau's sides and asked him to trot. *Keep him steady.*

Beau trotted with ease over the first three ground poles, and we hopped right over the first cross rail. He took a single canter stride before going over another ground pole and then did one canter stride before another one.

There was no time to even second-guess myself, because we popped over a cross rail, and with every stride, we went over a ground pole until Beau leaped over the final vertical.

"Nice work!" Rebecca called.

I trotted Beau back to our teammates. Mila, Thea, Keir, and Emery all smiled at me while Selly and Nina looked bored.

"Good first round, everyone," Rebecca said. "Remember, I want to see you creating impulsion without adding speed. Even stride lengths are paramount here too. Let's add some height and go again."

While Rebecca set up the new jumps, I caught Thea's eye.

She smiled at me, and it hit me how much I'd missed that smile. I was going to talk to her and Vivi. *Today.*

After our lesson, I cooled out Beau and praised him for a good job. We made slow, easy loops around the arena, and I almost jumped in the saddle when Mila edged Circe over toward us.

"Good practice," Mila said.

"Very," I said. "You're fitting in so well on our team."

"Thanks." Mila gave Circe more rein, and the mare stretched her neck. "Speaking of our team and that conversation with Selly earlier, I wanted to make sure we were . . . um, *friends* before we go to Canterwood. I don't want Selly coming after us because she thinks we're not totally focused on the team."

I nodded. "Right." I started stumbling over my words. "Y-yeah. Friends."

"Cool," Mila said, a flicker of something in her eye. "Hey, did you have fun with your, um, other friend at the dance? I didn't see you two together."

"She couldn't make it," I blurted out.

"Oh." Mila gave me a small smile. "Sorry."

"I saw you dancing with someone," I said.

"That was Ellie," Mila said. "We had fun."

I managed to hold back tears and nodded. I couldn't get out any words, but Mila led Circe away, saving me from having to try.

The second my "friend" was out of earshot, I let out a long sigh. I did *not* want to be Mila's friend. But I also couldn't get in her way with Ellie. I wanted Mila to be happy—even if that didn't mean with me. Plus, having her firmly in the friend zone was better than her hating me, right?

"We have a new friend, boy," I grumbled to Beau.

Great. But at least if Mila was into another girl, and not me, I could still be her friend. Even if it hurt.

Tell Me What's Up

AFTER DINNER, I COULDN'T WAIT ANY
longer. I'd put it off long enough, and it was
time to talk to my friends. Before I could change
my mind, I went to my group text with Thea and Vivi and
typed a message.

Abby: I need to talk to you both. Are you busy?

My phone chimed once. Then again.

Vivi: I'm free!

Thea: Me too. Riverfront gazebo in ten?

I almost couldn't believe they'd texted me back so fast.

"Wish me luck, friends," I whispered to my plants as I tugged on shoes and then headed out.

My heart thumped hard in my chest as I neared the gazebo. Thea and Vivi stood inside, waiting for me. They smiled when they saw me, and I managed a wobbly smile back.

"Hey," I said, stepping inside. "Thanks for meeting me."

"Of course," Vivi said. "Your text made me worry a little."

Thea nodded. "Yeah, is everything okay?"

I sighed, tears threatening to spill down my cheeks. "I don't know. That's why I wanted to talk to you two." I took a deep breath. "It feels like we're falling apart! I know you're both angry with me for some reason, and I get it if you're still mad about the Selly secret, but it really hurts being iced out."

Thea and Vivi looked at each other, then back at me.

"Abby, I'm sorry," Vivi said. "I promise—I wasn't mad about the Selly thing. I understand why you didn't tell us. And honestly? I probably would have done the same."

"But you and Thea are avoiding me!" I cried. "And making plans without me!"

Thea's face fell. "That's my fault. Not Vivi's. I asked her to keep a secret for me."

"What?" I asked.

"It's about Cora," Thea said. "Last night, I finally begged her to let me tell you, too, and she said yes. When you texted me, I was like, perfect, I can finally tell Abby!" Thea took a deep breath. "She's been struggling at school. She thought it was going to be great coming here, but it's been tough on her. She was thinking of leaving, actually."

"Oh no," I said. "I'm sorry. But what does that have to do with Vivi?"

"Well, at first, I didn't know that I wasn't supposed to tell anyone," Thea said. "So, I told Vivi because I knew Cora was interested in theater, and I thought if she talked to Vivi, maybe Vivi would introduce her to some new people and get her involved. That it would make her want to stay."

"That was a great idea," I said.

Thea smiled. "I thought so too. But Cora was super mad at me for telling someone. Even Vivi. She made me swear not to tell anyone else that she was having a hard time. She was so embarrassed. I told her there was nothing to be ashamed about, but she was."

"But Thea had already told me," Vivi said, "so I met up with her and Cora a couple of times. We went to the theater, and I introduced her to some kids her age."

That explained the Instagram post.

"We're so sorry, Abby," Thea said. "I've been so distracted and worried about Cora. If I'm not with her, I'm texting her or talking to her. I don't want her to go home. She's dreamed about coming to Saddlehill, and I know she wants to be here. It's just scary at first."

"I wanted to tell you so bad!" Vivi said. "But I didn't want to betray Cora's trust. And that day we had lunch plans? Those were with Cora. I *hated* not telling you! And I'm so sorry you thought our friendships were messed up or that you'd done something wrong."

Tears burned my eyes. "So . . . you both don't hate me?"

"Um, not at all!" Thea said.

She and Vivi reached out and hugged me as relief ran through my body. I wasn't mad at them. I would have done everything to protect Cora too, especially if she was feeling so awful.

On shaky legs, I went over to a bench and sat down. Thea hurried to sit on one side of me, and Vivi sat on the other.

"Is Cora doing any better?" I asked, wiping my eyes.

"A little," Thea said. "She likes the theater kids, and she's starting to make friends."

"That's great," I said, smiling softly at Thea. "She's lucky to have you." I looked over at Vivi. "And you, too. It sounds like you gave her something to look forward to."

"I think Cora thought riding was all she needed when she got here," Thea said, "and when she realized there's a bit of separation between Foxbury and Saddlehill, she felt lost."

"I hate that for her. Has she talked to your parents?" I asked.

Thea shook her head. "She said she knows how much they sacrificed to send us both here, so she doesn't want them to think she's ungrateful, even though I told her she wasn't."

"I wish she'd talk to them," I said. "But you can't force her."

"No, or she'll hide stuff from me," Thea said. "As long as she's talking to me, I told her I'll keep it to myself."

"You're a great sister," I said.

Maybe one day I could be half as good a sister to Emery.

The three of us looked at each other, and it felt like I had my best friends back. That all the secrets were out in the open, and there was nothing in our way now.

"I was so hurt because I thought you two were ditching me and becoming closer," I said. "And I want you to be great friends! Just . . . don't forget about me."

"Never," Thea said firmly.

"Ever," Vivi added.

"So, we're okay?" I asked them.

"We're very okay," Vivi said.

Thea nodded. "We're *good*."

We group hugged, and my body felt limp with relief.

"Now that we're talking again," Thea said, "what's going on with you and Mila? You didn't even dance with her in Salem!"

I sighed. "It's kind of a long story."

"Want to tell us over ice cream?" Vivi asked.

"Definitely," I said.

Together, the three of us left the gazebo, and all felt right in my world again.

Dear Sasha
and Heather

BY THE TIME WEDNESDAY ROLLED around, I was so ready to get on the road to Canterwood that I almost couldn't stand it! Yesterday Thea and I had gone shopping together after school and had found all the clothing and items we needed for the Canterwood costume contest. We'd decided to enter as a pair, and I couldn't wait for everyone to see what we'd chosen to wear!

There was so much to do before leaving tomorrow. While Vivi slept, I tiptoed around our room and started laying out my clothes—both for everyday and for riding—to pack. Plus, emergency outfits in case something happened to my breeches or shirts.

"Abby, what're you doing?" Vivi asked, peering out from under her floral comforter. She slept with her head covered. Probably for the same reason I always made sure my feet were under blankets at night. Monsters!

"I'm sorry!" I said, wincing. "I tried to be quiet, but I wanted to do some packing this morning, so I didn't have to do it all tonight."

Vivi waved her hand. "You were totally fine. I knew my alarm was about to go off." She sat up and rubbed her eyes as she surveyed the piles of clothes I'd made on my bed and on my side of the room. "How long have you been awake?"

"A couple of hours. But look." I held up one of my show shirts, frowning. "There's a stain on this that I did *not* see when I washed it last. So, I can't wear that one. And my other one's"—I shrugged—"somewhere. But I can't find it."

"Give me your dirty shirt, and I bet I can get the stain out," Vivi said. "And if you want, I'll look for your other shirt in your closet after school. You'll be at the stable then, right?"

I nodded. "Gotta pack up Beau."

"Okay. Then I'll help pack you. You can keep making piles of clothes to take, or text me a list of what you want, and I'll find it in your stuff."

"You're the best. Thank you."

"No problem," Vivi said, smiling. "I wish I could come!"

I pouted. "Me too! We need to figure out how to get permission for you to skip school and go next time."

"Maybe I should tell everyone I'm your emotional support best friend. Then they'd say yes!"

I laughed. "You know, that might work. We'll have to try it."

Vivi slid out of bed and padded off to get cleaned up for school.

"Five more minutes," I told myself. Then I had to get ready too.

My classes dragged, but by lunch, I was free, and my four-day weekend started. I waited for Thea outside her math class, and she grinned when she saw me.

"We made it!" she said. "We're officially done with school for the week. I love getting out early for shows!"

"Me too!" I said. "Not a moment too soon."

Thea nodded. "Let's go grab lunch, and then we can get changed and go to the barn."

Together, we headed to the cafeteria. We both got chicken sandwiches, waffle fries, and Cokes. We snagged our usual table by the big bay window, and I dove into my fries first.

"Who are we riding with to Canterwood?" I asked. "Allie?"

"Probably?" Thea shrugged. "Or Rebecca. Unless she drives one of the trailers, but I bet she has Kaitlin and Peter drive."

They were two head grooms at Foxbury.

"You better sit next to me," I said. "I don't want to be trapped in the car with Selly or Nina inches away from me."

"No one wants that," Thea said.

We focused on our food, and all I could think about was my giant to-do list for today and tomorrow morning.

Later that evening, Thea and I armed ourselves with snacks and drinks and settled into my room to work on our applications for the winter clinic. I was at my desk and Thea had borrowed Vivi's since she was out. We were at it for over an hour, because writing a letter to Sasha and Heather was *hard*.

"Ugh," I groaned. "I've hit my backspace key so many times, I'm surprised it still works."

"Tell me about it," Thea said. "I think I'm going to set a

timer for twenty minutes and just write. No stopping until the alarm goes off. And then I'll see what I've got after that."

"Okay, I'll try that too," I said. "Why not?"

"Timer set," Thea said, "and *go*!"

I took a deep breath and forced my fingers to move over the keyboard. It was hard to get started, but once I got into it, I forgot about the timer, and instead, I lost myself in the letter.

After what seemed like no time at all, Thea's computer dinged.

"Time's up," Thea said, cracking her knuckles. "How'd you do?"

"Great, actually! How about you?"

"The sprint worked better than I thought," Thea said. "I got a lot done."

"Sweet! Want to do one more? I think I can finish then."

Thea nodded. "Let's do it."

She set her timer again, and we got going. My fingers flew over the keys, and twenty minutes later, I typed the final sentence of my letter as Thea's alarm beeped.

"Done!" I said.

She looked over at me from Vivi's desk. "Me too!"

"Can I hear yours?" I asked her.

"Of course!" Thea put her laptop in her lap and spun around in Vivi's desk chair to face me.

She read me her letter, which talked about how she and Chaos were dedicated members of Foxbury's riding team and how this clinic would be a great opportunity for them to grow their skills.

"'And that's why I hope you pick us,'" Thea read. "'We're ready to work hard, and I'd love to learn from two amazing riders. Thank you for your consideration. Warmly, Thea Song.'"

"It's perfect!" I said. "Gah, they're so going to pick you!"

Thea shimmied her shoulders. "I hope so! Read me yours!"

"Okay, okay," I said, scrolling to the top of my page. "Here we go."

> Dear Sasha and Heather,
> My name is Abby St. Clair, and I'm a rider in seventh grade at Saddlehill Academy. I ride for Foxbury Stables with my horse Beau, and we're on the middle novice team. I grew up

watching you both compete, and it's
surreal that I'm writing to you now.
Like me, you both started your careers
riding while in middle school. In high
school, you competed all over the US
and Europe, which is what I want to
do. I'm such a nerd that I have your
dates for the Olympic Trials on my
calendar, and if I can, I'll be there
to cheer you both on. At the risk of
sounding like a suck-up, I'm a big fan.

I took a breath.

If I get accepted to your clinic, I'll
work to become a well-rounded rider
who can excel in three-day eventing,
just like you two. I want to compete
for the United States Equestrian Team
one day and ride in the Olympics. If I
attend the clinic, I'll be able to learn
from two successful riders who are

on that track. I hope you'll consider
me for a spot. Attending this clinic
would be one of the best things to ever
happen to me. Thank you so much.
All the best, Abby St. Clair

I looked up from my computer to meet Thea's eyes. "Is it okay?" I asked.

"It's more than okay," Thea said with a soft smile. "It's great, Abs. You have to get in. Sasha and Heather could mentor you and help you get to the Olympics."

"I'd *die* if I got in," I said.

"Me too! But we would have to be brought back to life so we could actually go!" Thea said, laughing.

"True, true. Want to film our intros? I'm glad you decided to do one too."

"It was a great idea," Thea said. "Let's do it."

Thea grabbed her phone while I finger-combed my hair and straightened my shirt. She aimed the camera at me. "Whenever you're ready!"

I took a deep breath through my nose. "Hi, I'm Abby St. Clair! This is part of my application video for your winter riding clinic. I'm so excited to send you a brief video! My letter is also included in my submission. Thank you both so much for considering me. I hope to meet you this winter!"

I waited a beat, then nodded.

"Perfect," Thea said. "Do mine?"

She handed me her phone, and I filmed her introduction.

Then we edited everything and attached the videos to our emails to Sasha and Heather.

"Should we send them?" I asked, my hands shaking.

"Yes, but ahhh," Thea said. "This is so nerve-racking!"

We laughed, shaking our heads at ourselves. It felt like I was about to jump off a high dive!

"On three?" I asked.

Thea nodded. "On three."

"One," I said.

"Two," Thea said.

"Three!" we said together.

I pressed send, and the email that determined my whole future whooshed away to Sasha and Heather.

"AHHH!" I yelled, slamming my computer lid closed.

"We did it!" Thea said. She copied me and shut her laptop.

"I know we have to pack," I said. "But, like, I need a walk

or something first. I'll never be able to focus, otherwise."

Thea nodded, and we hurried out of my room, giggling.

A while later, I flopped face-first onto my bed. Everything was done. My stuff was packed. Beau's things were ready. I'd showered *and* used a hair mask.

All I needed now was to get to sleep soon, since I had to be up extra early tomorrow. But before I slept, I was supposed to FaceTime Dad. He'd texted me while I'd been at the stable, and I'd promised I would call when I got back in my room.

Still lying on my stomach, I raised myself onto my elbows and called him. Vivi had earbuds in and was finishing a movie, so I knew I wouldn't bother her.

"There's my girl!" Dad said after answering. He smiled and put his glasses up on top of his head. "How are you, sweetie?"

"Good! Tired, but I got everything done," I said.

Dad nodded. "I can imagine how wiped you are. Are you going to get some sleep soon?"

"Once we hang up. I set, like, four alarms, and Vivi even turned on hers, so I'm completely sure I won't miss getting up on time."

"When do you need to be up?"

"Four thirty," I said. "Gotta go to the stable, get Beau's shipping boots on, and get him loaded. The trailers leave at six."

"I see all the work you're doing, honey," Dad said. "And I'm so proud of you. I know you're going to Canterwood for a show, but I want you to have fun, too."

"I will. That's kind of why we're going up early. There's a party tomorrow evening with the other riders, and I'm hoping to get a tour of Canterwood's campus."

Dad grinned. "Well, that would be something you'd remember forever, I bet. Checking out the former home of Sasha and Lauren."

"And Heather." I made a face. "And *Jasmine King*."

Dad knew all about my favorite and not-favorite riders. I talked about them a lot and even got him interested in some of their show standings. Plus, he'd promised to take me to one of the pre-Olympic trials where they'd be riding, so I wanted him to know who they were before we went next year.

"I'm sure you'll have a fantastic time," Dad said. "And I expect to receive tons of pictures from you and Emery."

"Absolutely. We'll text you when we get there."

Dad and I talked for a couple more minutes before saying

good night and hanging up. I flicked off my light and snuggled deep under my blankets. Ever since things had gone back to normal with Thea and Vivi, I'd been trying to figure out what to do about Mila. I wanted to tell her *everything*. And now that I was sure I'd done nothing to make my best friends hate me, I finally had the brain space to wonder if Mila and I could be more than friends.

I'd talk to her after the show. But until then, I wanted to make it up to her for the way I'd iced her out. And maybe, just maybe, we'd still have a chance at being something more than friends.

Too Early for Violence

MY ALARM JOLTED ME AWAKE AT four thirty the next morning. I didn't even scroll my socials like I usually did before I got up. Instead, I threw off my covers and hurried over to grab my clothes off my desk chair and get dressed.

Vivi peered at me from under her blanket. "Need anything?"

"Nope, go back to sleep."

I tugged off my pajamas and pulled on jeans and an old Foxbury sweatshirt.

"'Kay. Good luck, and you better FaceTime me when you walk on the same ground as Sasha and Lauren."

I grinned. "Will do!"

Vivi snuggled into her pillow. "Don't bring home any dirt or rocks or grass from Canterwood. There's no room in here with all your plants."

That made me snort. "Noted."

A few minutes later, I was at the bus stop with my suitcase at my feet. It was dark except for the well-lit parking lot, and I shivered in the cold.

I turned around as the unmistakable sound of other suit-cases rolling on the pavement got my attention.

Thea, Selly, Nina, and Emery trudged down the sidewalk and over to me. Keir was a few steps behind them. Selly's usu-ally perfect hair was flat on one side and sticking up at funny angles on the other.

"What?" she snapped, getting a look at my face. "I didn't have time to do my hair this morning."

"I can see that," I said. I twisted away from Selly as she tried to hit my arm.

"Please stop," Nina said. "It's too early for violence."

That made us all laugh a little. Even Selly.

"Morning," I said to Emery.

She smiled at me. "Hey. I'm dead right now, but I know I'll perk up once I see Bliss."

"Oh, me too," I said. "We all kinda messed up, though. Someone should have taken one for the team and gone for Starbucks."

"We should DoorDash it to the stable!" Selly said, her brown eyes widening. "If we order it now . . ."

"It'll be at Foxbury when we get there!" I said.

"Let's do it," Selly said. "I'm desperate. This *once* I'll order for everyone. You can get me something next time, okay?"

"Deal," Thea said.

The rest of us nodded. I could count on one hand the number of nice things Selly had ever done for me. This was by far the very best thing she'd ever done!

We'd just finished ordering our teas, hot chocolates, and lattes by the time the Saddlehill bus pulled up. The driver climbed off the bus and helped us load our stuff. Then we were off!

A few minutes later, we arrived at Foxbury to complete and utter chaos. Pulling our suitcases behind us, we headed for the main barn, dodging riders and horses.

"Has anyone seen my shipping boots?" an older girl asked. "I can't find them!"

A guy shook his head. "No, but have you seen Cara? My bridle is gone!"

Cara was an instructor for some of the advanced riders.

"These people act like they've never been to a show before," Selly grumbled under her breath.

"Whatever," Nina said. "The second I'm in the car, I'm sleeping."

We took our suitcases over to a stack of other luggage waiting to be loaded, and as we were about to duck into the barn, a car pulled in. A tall guy emerged from the car with two cardboard beverage holders, both filled with cups.

"Oh my god, you made it," Selly said. She practically ran up to him and grabbed the cup with her name on it. "I was about to go to sleep in a *stall*." She huffed. "And sheesh. Do I look like someone who would sleep in a barn?" She handed me one of the drink trays. "Abby would!" she added.

I couldn't argue with her. She had me there.

Once everyone had their hot drinks, we all split up and headed to get our horses ready. I made my way down the aisle, looking for Mila so I could say good morning and give her the caramel latte I'd ordered. I'd go dig a Coke out of the fridge for caffeine, but I wanted her to have something warm.

I hurried toward Circe's stall and spotted Mila kneeling in front of her tack trunk.

"I brought you some caffeine," I said.

Mila's head popped up. "You did?" She eyed the cup. "You sure you're not a mirage? I'm tired enough this morning that I'm not sure you're real."

Laughing, I handed Mila the drink. "That convince you of my realness yet?" I asked.

Mila took a sip. "Mmm, yup. Thank you. I needed this. Especially since Circe's in a mood."

I peered through the iron bars into the mare's stall. She paced back and forth from one end of the stall to the other, flicking her tail angrily.

"Hey, girl," I said softly. "It's okay. Shhh."

Circe didn't look at me. Or listen. Instead, she pinned her ears and kept pacing.

"Is she going to be okay to travel?" I asked.

Mila winced. "I hope so. I kinda need her to compete, you know?"

"What? You mean you can't take those jumps by yourself?"

"Nope, but maybe next year!"

We smiled tentatively at each other.

"When you're ready to load her, come find me if you want," I said. "We'll lead her out, and I know the grooms will help."

Mila brushed strands of her long red hair off her forehead. "I have a feeling I'm going to need all the help I can get. I may lunge her first if she doesn't settle down."

"That's a great idea."

After I was sure Mila didn't need anything else, I headed for the stable fridge, and once a soda was in hand, I hurried to Beau's stall. Unlike Circe, he was half asleep and seemed completely oblivious to everything going on around him.

"Time to wake up," I whispered. "It's travel day!"

Nothing. Not even a flick of an ear in my direction or a slow blink of an eye.

I pouted. "Well, I had this *treat* for you. But I guess I'll take it back, since you're too sleepy to eat it."

In an instant, Beau's eyes popped open, and he lumbered toward me, sniffing.

"Oh, wow," I said. "You woke up just in time. It's a miracle."

I dug into my hoodie pocket and produced an apple molasses cookie, which I put on my flattened palm and held out to Beau. He lipped up the treat, his soft whiskers tickling my hand.

He munched happily, and I dug out his grooming kit from his tack trunk. I wanted to keep him as calm as possible, so I was going to brush him in his stall this morning.

I sped through grooming Beau, and once he was extra shiny and clean, I grabbed his shipping boots and got his legs wrapped.

"I'm going to go find Rebecca before I take you out, boy," I said. "I want to make sure she's ready for you first. Be right back."

I weaved my way down the aisle, looking for Rebecca. Finally, I spotted her outside in the parking lot. She stood behind three giant horse trailers and was talking to Allie.

"Hey, Abby," Rebecca said. "You ready to go soon?"

"Yup! Just checking to see when you want me to bring out Beau."

Rebecca checked her phone. "We should start loading in a few minutes. Why don't you go get Beau, and we'll get him loaded with one of the first groups."

"Okay, be right back," I said.

I hurried to Beau's stall and clipped his lead line to his halter. "It's time! You ready?"

Beau blinked at me and bobbed his head.

Together, we walked down the aisle and back toward Rebecca and Allie.

"Do you want someone to load him, Abby?" Allie asked, walking over to us.

"I can do it," I said. "It's good practice for me."

Allie nodded. "You got this. Remember, be calm and assertive."

Taking a deep breath, I turned Beau in a large circle and let him get a look at the trailer. He didn't seem fazed by it, and his posture was relaxed, with ears flicking gently back and forth and tail swishing slowly.

We made one more circle, and then I led him up to the trailer at an easy walk. "Let's go, boy," I said. I kept him close to me on a short line. "Time to get in."

Beau lowered his head to sniff the metal, then took a cautious, careful step up.

"Good job!" I told him. "Come on. Hop in all the way."

Gently, I tugged on his halter, and he climbed inside. I petted his neck and praised him as Allie walked in and helped me get him secured inside.

"Nice work, Abby," Allie said as we got out of the trailer.

I smiled. "Thanks! Beau makes it easy."

While Allie and Rebecca loaded more horses, I went to look over all the stuff in Beau's tack trunk. After double-checking the list on my phone, I was sure I'd packed all the essentials last night. I wheeled Beau's trunk to the front of the stable so the grooms could help me load it when they were ready.

My eye caught on a flash of gray-and-lavender shipping boots. Circe pranced around Mila as she tried to calm her horse down. I hurried over to them and clipped my spare lead line onto Circe's halter.

"Thank you," Mila said, sweat beading along her hairline. "Rebecca said someone else would take her, but I want to at least walk her myself."

Together, Mila and I walked Circe up and down the grassy edge of the parking lot. The mare's neck darkened with sweat as she jigged between us, nostrils flaring pink as she watched the different horses being loaded. But Mila stayed calm and focused on Circe. After a couple more minutes of walking, Rebecca waved us over.

"Let's get her in, Mila," Rebecca said. "I'll take her now, okay?"

"Sure," Mila said.

I unclipped my lead line, and Mila handed hers to Rebecca. Stepping back, I crossed my fingers that Circe would load easily.

Rebecca circled her once, then moved closer to Circe's head and started the mare at a quick walk toward the trailer.

"Come on," Rebecca said. "Let's go in."

But Circe halted, digging in her heels and flattening her ears.

"We've done so much trailering practice," Mila said, groaning.

"Rebecca's got her," I said. "Don't worry yet."

Rebecca circled Circe away from the trailer, talking in a calm voice, and then led her right back to it.

Allie hurried over and patted Circe's rump encouragingly. "C'mon," she said. "In you go."

Circe shuddered, and I grimaced, sure she was going to yank Rebecca backward and cause them to circle again. But the mare scrambled up into the trailer, nearly stepping on Rebecca in her hurry to get inside.

"She's in! She's in!" Mila cheered.

We high-fived. "Told you!" I said.

So far, things were going right today! Maybe it was a sign that this show would be a good one. A girl could hope.

Canterwood Crest Academy

"A BBY, IF YOU TOUCH ME AGAIN, I'M going to scream," Selly growled from the seat next to me.

I was in the middle of the backseat of Allie's tiny car, with Thea on one side and Selly on the other. The rest of our team was in Rebecca's SUV. Most unfortunately for me, Rebecca had determined our seating arrangements.

We'd been on the road for a couple of hours, and we still had about an hour to go until we reached Canterwood. It was slower going with horse trailers, but we hadn't hit any major traffic as we'd left Foxbury and got on the highway toward Connecticut.

"I'm sorry," I said. "It's not like I'm doing it on purpose. But we're next to each other in the backseat of a car. My arm *will* occasionally brush yours."

Selly dug around in the quilted black mini-backpack at her feet and pulled out oversized sunglasses. She put them on and stared out the window, not looking at me anymore, which was fine with me.

I pulled out my phone and started a text.

Abby: How's it going over there?

Immediately, Emery wrote back.

Emery: Good! Except for Nina locking eyes with me and telling me I better win for the team "or else."

Abby: Yaaaay, aren't you glad you joined our team??

Emery: Hahaha, right?? I was just like, I'll do my best! And she did NOT like that answer lol

Abby: Maybe she'll pull a Selly and refuse to look at you because you brushed her arm by accident. Try it!

We texted for a few more minutes before I put my phone away and laid my head back. A few minutes of a nap wouldn't be the worst thing in the world. Next to me, Thea was snoring gently, and I couldn't tell if Selly had passed out or not, but she wasn't moving.

Go to sleep, I told myself. *When you wake up, you'll be at Canterwood.*

"Hey, sleeping beauties," Allie said sometime later. "We're here!"

I opened one eye but started to fall back asleep. Too tired. I was so cozy, and the hum of the car lulled me to sleep.

But then.

I remembered.

CANTERWOOD!

That did it! I was very awake in two seconds flat. Rubbing the sleep from my eyes, I caught Allie's eye in the rearview mirror.

"We made it!" I cheered.

Thea and Selly were awake now too, and I practically climbed into Thea's lap so I could look out the window as we slow-rolled through ivy-covered wrought-iron gates.

I grabbed Thea's upper arm and squeezed. "Thea," I whispered. "Are you sure about this?"

"Too late to back out now," she said, her voice hushed. "We're here!"

I couldn't help but wonder how Sasha and Lauren had felt as they'd come through these very gates to become superstar equestrians at Canterwood Crest Academy. I doubted that they'd been as nervous as I'd been when I'd first pulled into Saddlehill.

I tried to take a deep breath, but instead, I swallowed air wrong and coughed.

"Could you not, like, die before we show?" Selly snapped.

I rolled my eyes, then focused on the campus as we pulled into the parking lot. When we came to a stop, I practically pushed Thea out of the car so I could get out.

"Abs, we're gonna be here for a while!" Thea said, laughing.

"I know, but"—I took a deep breath of Canterwood Crest air—"I don't want to miss a second!"

I spun in a slow circle, taking in every square inch of the campus that I could see from here. The gorgeous stone buildings, the beautiful rolling hills, and the dark-lacquered stable seated back off the parking lot.

"Smile!" Thea said, standing in front of me with her phone out. "I'm going to document this moment for you!"

I grinned like an idiot for the camera. Then I pulled Thea over beside me, and we took a selfie.

We were still looking around, open-mouthed in awe, when

the horse trailers pulled in behind us. Everyone got to work unloading the horses, and it wasn't long before the trailers were empty.

"Why don't you kids go find your horses' stalls," Rebecca said, "and we'll start removing your tack trunks."

My eyes widened. "You—you want us to go by ourselves? Like, *alone*?"

Rebecca smiled and winked at me. "You'll be fine. Promise."

"It's just another stable," Selly said, shaking her head. "It's not like we're gonna see Sasha or Lauren or *any* of the famous riders from here."

"You never know!" I protested.

"Except we kinda do!" Selly snapped. "They don't even go here now!"

"Girls." Rebecca's tone was firm and carried a hint of a warning.

Selly and I shot her sheepish looks but closed our mouths, and we turned toward the stable.

Together, we led our horses down a grassy path. There were signs directing riders in the right direction.

"I can't believe we're here," I said to Thea. I'd been talking her ear off since we'd arrived.

"It does feel unbelievable!" she said.

I glanced behind us at Mila and Circe, and the gray mare walked calmly beside Mila as if she'd been that relaxed the entire day. But whew. I was glad she wasn't tearing Mila's arms off.

Beau tugged on his lead line, yanking me forward. "Heeey," I said. "No pulling."

The paddocks around us practically gleamed in the sun, and every blade of grass was clipped to *exactly* the same height. Like someone had gotten out a ruler and made sure it was all even.

Behind us, a car backfired in the parking lot, and Beau snorted and hopped sideways. *No!* He almost tugged the lead line through my hands, but I caught the end of it just in time.

"Beau!" I hissed. "Calm down, boy."

I could imagine him galloping away from me at top speed, lead line dangling between his legs. Ugh, he could even have scared another horse and made a rider fall off or something. That would have been a *nightmare*! Especially on our first day at Canterwood!

"This place isn't that great," Nina said. She walked Adore next to me and Beau. "Foxbury is prettier."

"I think they're both nice," Keir said. He led Magic on a loose lead line ahead of me.

Nina rolled her eyes but didn't say anything else.

We took the horses up to the stable and stared, unsure where to go next.

"Welcome, riders!" I turned toward the smooth voice of a guy with deep brown skin and a shock of jet-black hair walking over to us, smiling. He had the warmest brown eyes I'd ever seen.

"I'm Eric Rodriguez," he said, "and I'm a former student turned assistant instructor here at Canterwood. We're glad to have you all!"

He looked like he was around Sasha's age.

"Thank you!" I said. "Um, did you know Sasha?" I blurted it out before I could stop myself.

"I'm sorry about her, Eric," Selly said. "Abby doesn't get out much."

My face went red, and I wanted to melt into the ground.

But Eric waved one of his hands. "It's all right. I get why you'd ask. And yes, I knew Sasha. Still do, in fact. We're really good friends."

I blinked, staring at him. "Wow," I finally said.

Eric laughed. "What stable are you from? Then I can point you toward the right stall block."

"We're from Foxbury," Thea said proudly.

Eric studied the clipboard in his hands. "Ah, yup. Okay, you'll find your stalls at the back of the main barn. They're all labeled."

The. Main. Barn.

My brain started to short-circuit. I'd figured that barn would be full, or they'd send us to a second or third smaller barn and keep the central stable for Canterwood horses. But nope!

"If you need anything, come grab me," Eric said. "I'm always around. And if you can't get ahold of me, you can also reach out to my boss, Mr. Conner. He's the head instructor here. Our numbers are on a contact sheet you'll find on a table outside my office. Grab one before you leave today."

We nodded.

"Thank you," Keir said. "We'll go get our horses put up."

Eric nodded. "Cool. And"—he checked his phone—"once you're all settled, I'm going to be giving a tour of the campus before lunch. If you're interested, you can meet me here at eleven thirty."

Excited looks passed among me and my teammates.

"We'll be here," Selly said.

The rest of us nodded, and I hid a laugh. Miss Ew, This Campus Is So Boring was suddenly down for a tour.

"Great," Eric said. "I'll see you later, then."

He headed off toward another group of riders who had just arrived on campus.

"Let's go get the horses settled," Keir said. He led the way into the stable, and the rest of us followed behind him.

We walked our horses down the main aisle, looking for notes about which stalls were ours. At the end of the aisle, just like Eric had said, we found sticky notes on the stall doors.

"Here's Adore's," I said.

"And Bliss is over here," Thea said, pointing.

"Beau's on this side!" Mila said. "Next to Circe."

I led Beau over toward Mila and Circe, smiling. "Yay!"

We worked to get the horses settled, and I tried not to be overwhelmed from being here. On this campus. At this school!

"Well, look who it is," someone said in a velvety smooth voice outside Beau's stall.

I looked out over the stall door and smiled at Olivia. Her BFF Ava was next to her. They were both dressed in nearly identical riding outfits, from spotless breeches to hoodies without horsehair on them.

Selly, Thea, Nina, and I emerged from our horses' stalls seconds apart.

Olivia smiled at us, flashing perfect teeth. "It's the Foxbury Four!"

"Actually," Mila said, popping her head over Circe's stall door, "there are seven of us on our team, and we're all here. So, we probably need a different nickname."

"Whatever you call yourselves, welcome to Canterwood," Ava said. She sized us up, taking in the competition.

"Thanks," Selly said coolly. The rest of my team nodded.

The Canterwood riders traded glances with each other, looking like they wanted to say something else, but they turned away from us.

"See you at the party!" Olivia called back.

I stared after them as they walked away, wondering how tonight would go.

Eric the Tour Guide

LATER THAT MORNING, WE'D FINISHED getting the horses settled into their temporary new home and had given them some light exercise after traveling. Rebecca, Allie, Kaitlin, and Peter had helped us all unload our tack trunks, and we'd carried some of our other stuff into a spare room in the main barn.

While we were getting our Canterwood tour, Rebecca had gone to the local hotel to check us in and grab the key cards for our rooms. After we finished up with Eric, we were all going back to the hotel to unwind for a bit and get ready for the party later.

"How're you doing?" Emery asked, walking over to stand by me. "I know coming here means a lot to you."

"It's still very surreal," I said. "It's almost like a dream. As if I've been here before. This campus feels familiar for some reason I can't quite explain, and it's *weird*."

"Maybe you're tied to Sasha or Lauren in some way you don't know about," she said. "The universe can be clever like that!"

I smiled. "Maybe! Whatever it is, I'm just glad to be here."

Eric headed in our direction. "Ready to go?" he asked us.

"Ready," I said.

Everyone else nodded.

With that, we followed him away from the stable, and I clutched my phone, trying not to take a picture of every single building I passed. Eric pointed out some of the residence halls—Yule, Hollis, and Reynolds.

"And over there is the famed Winchester Hall," he said, "where Sasha lived for a while."

My eyes widened. Sasha had lived *there*?!

"But," Eric whispered, "there's a secret about that dorm."

"What?" Nina asked.

"The *real* name of the hall, the one that residents try never to speak of, is Winchester A. Butkis Hall."

"Nooo," Mila said. "No way!"

Everyone giggled. That was the worst hall name ever!

Eric shook his head. "Can't imagine growing up with that last name. Poor Mr. Butkis probably had it rough in school."

Giggling, we kept walking, and Eric gave us a great tour, showing us the gym, cafeteria, and media center.

"So, you went to Canterwood, right?" Thea asked Eric.

"Yup," he said. "Same graduating class as Heather and Sasha."

"And now you're a riding instructor here," Thea said. "That's pretty cool. Did you go to college or start teaching right away?"

"After high school, I attended the University of Virginia," he said.

"Where's that?" Selly asked.

"Charlottesville," Eric said. "And Sasha, Heather, and Callie all went to Hollins University, which is only a couple hours away in Roanoke."

I knew Callie was Sasha's best friend, and they'd gone to Canterwood together.

"We made our schools' riding teams too," Eric continued. "I studied history and got a degree in that, thinking I wanted to be a professor." Eric chuckled. "But then I was visiting Canterwood a few years ago to chat with prospective students, and I started talking to Mr. Conner. He asked me to come back to Canterwood and instruct here, so I did." He smiled. "And now, I can't imagine doing anything else."

Eric had the best energy. I really liked him, and I bet his riders did too.

We walked down the sidewalk, and Eric pointed out the English, history, and science buildings. The campus was more spread out than Saddlehill's, and I was glad not to have to walk so far to get everywhere like students did here.

"Did you apply to the winter clinic?" Eric asked, catching my eye.

I nodded. "The second applications were open!"

"I almost wish I could have applied," he said. "Being taught by Sasha *and* Heather? You're gonna learn so much! Those two are experts, so whatever they have to say, listen."

"If I get in," I said. "I'm sure there were a lot of applicants. More than last year, probably."

"Still, you never know if you don't try. Sasha used to teach it by herself, but she wanted to keep expanding and working with more riders, so that's why she asked her girlfriend to instruct with her. They work so well together, and riders come away with a great education."

"Learning from them would be the best," I said. "Cross your fingers for me!"

Eric grinned and held up his left hand with fingers crossed. "You got it!"

After the fantastic tour, we said goodbye to Eric and climbed into Rebecca's SUV to head to our hotel.

"Did everyone text their parents and let them know you're here safe?" Rebecca asked.

Mila and I traded grimaces. And so did all the other people in the SUV. Whoops!

"Okay then, when we're checked in, you'll text them," Rebecca said, shaking her head slightly.

We pulled up to the hotel and followed Rebecca inside. She and Allie had already put our bags in our rooms, which made them the best people ever! In the lobby, Rebecca handed each of us our room keys.

"The rooms are next to each other, and you *can* switch, but I tried to pair you with the right roomies," she said. "If you change rooms, you're responsible for moving your stuff."

We nodded.

"We've got two suites for you all," Rebecca said. "In one suite, we've got Nina and Selly. And in the other suite will be Abby, Thea, Mila, and Emery. Keir, you have a room all to yourself."

Yesss! I looked at my friends and grinned. This was *perfect*!

"Great," Selly said. "Thank you!"

The rest of us smiled.

"Allie and I have rooms next to yours," Rebecca said. "And before I let you loose, let's go over the ground rules."

I tried to pay attention, but all I could think about was getting into my suite with Emery and my friends. This was going to be like one long sleepover, and I was ready to get the party started!

". . . and no leaving the hotel without permission," Rebecca said. "If you want to go *anywhere*, you ask me first. Got it?"

"Got it," we all said.

"Good. Then you'll want to grab the elevator to the fifth floor and take a right. Go get settled, and then we'll figure out lunch."

"Let's go," Thea said, grabbing my hand.

Laughing, she tugged me toward the elevator. She, Mila,

Emery, and I crowded inside, and the doors started to close just as Selly was a few yards away.

"Hey!" Selly said sharply as she hurried over. "Wait!"

But it was too late. The doors closed on Selly's annoyed face, and we burst into giggles.

"She's totally going to get us back," I said.

"That's our problem for later," Mila said. "Right now, I want to get into our room and raid the mini-fridge!"

The elevator doors opened, and we spilled out into the hallway, looking for our suite number.

"Found it," Mila said. "Room 407."

I stuck my card into the slot, and when the light blinked green, I pushed down the door handle and stepped inside.

"Wow," I said. "This is *amazing*!"

The suite had an upstairs loft with two double beds and a workspace, and a downstairs with a small kitchen, living room, huge bathroom, and a pullout sofa bed. The sheets were crisp, the room smelled lemony fresh, and our suitcases were piled neatly inside.

I walked to the giant window, which overlooked downtown, and grinned. I dug my phone out of my pocket and snapped a pic.

We made it! I typed in a text to Dad. I added the pic and sent it.

Immediately, he wrote back: Great, hon! Perfect view!

Putting away my phone, I looked at my friends. "Since you're the newest member of our team," I said to Mila, "what do you all think about letting Mila choose first where she wants to sleep? Then Emery?"

Thea nodded. "Works for me!"

"I'll take the sofa bed," Mila said. "That way I can starfish in my sleep like always and not kick or hit someone."

We laughed.

Emery eyed me. "Want to share a bed?" she asked shyly.

"Sure!" I said. "That'll be fun."

Thea ran toward one of the double beds and dove into it. "That means I get my own bed! This one spoke to me!"

Emery and I claimed the other double bed, and I kicked off my shoes and plopped onto my side. Today had been long, from getting up early to the anxiety of making sure Beau and the other horses arrived safely on campus. But we were all here now, and it was time to relax before the Canterwood party.

"Let's unpack," Thea said. "I want to see everyone's outfits for tonight!"

I hopped off the bed and grabbed my suitcase. We had to look *amazing*!

Is She Kidding?!

REBECCA KNOCKED ON OUR DOOR A short while later, looking slightly dazed when she eyeballed the giant pile of clothes we'd made on my and Emery's bed as we tried to pick the perfect outfits for tonight's party.

"I made a reservation at a cool café for lunch," Rebecca said. "So, meet me down in the lobby in five and we'll head out."

We promised we would be right down.

"This," Thea said, waving her arm at the clothes, "is gonna

have to wait. I still have no idea how we're going to decide what to wear."

"What if we went in pajamas?" Emery said, laughing.

"Oh yeah," I said. "If I go in my matching Grogu sleep shirt and pj pants, I can guarantee I'll blend right in."

Giggling, we left our room and headed for the elevator.

"C'mon, are you saying it would be wrong if I wore my fuzzy slippers?" Mila asked. "We could all go in pajamas and pretend to be offended that no one else got the memo to dress for sleep."

"That's not the worst idea I've ever heard," Thea said.

Downstairs, we met up with Keir, Selly, Nina, Rebecca, and Allie. We followed our instructors out to the parking lot and climbed into Rebecca's SUV. A few minutes later, we pulled up to a beautiful brick building that seemed to be made mostly of windows. It was situated off the road and surrounded by trees and wildflowers.

"Elizabeth's Tea Café," I said, "you are so cute!"

Inside, a waitress took us to our table in the back of the restaurant, and it was like sitting in a greenhouse! The walls and ceiling were glass, and there were bird feeders everywhere outside and flowers growing all over the place. I almost missed my chair as I tried to sit down while taking in everything.

"Did you choose this restaurant for Abby?" Thea asked, wide-eyed as she glanced around. "Because I have a feeling we're going to have a hard time getting her out of here!"

Rebecca laughed. "You know, I didn't, but after I made the reservation, I did wonder if Abby would simply vanish into the gardens, never to be seen again."

"Surely I wouldn't be the first," I said. "This place is amazing!"

All the wooden tables were painted white, to give them a shabby chic feel, and the color scheme was muted earth tones and soft pastels.

Mila was across from me, Thea was on one side, and Emery was on the other. I'd successfully built a little barricade against Selly and Nina. We ordered our drinks—sodas and teas—and browsed the menu, which was full of delightful sandwiches, soups, and yummy-sounding desserts.

"Is everyone excited about tonight?" Rebecca asked. "A party at Canterwood sounds like fun to me."

I nodded along with everyone else.

"A little nervous," Emery said softly. "Meeting a bunch of new people can be overwhelming sometimes."

I gently elbowed her side. "You'll have plenty of friends there."

Emery smiled at me. "Thanks, Abby."

"I think it'll be fun," Thea said. "They're mostly riders we sort of know anyway from shows, but it could be cool to hang out with them in a less stressful situation than a competition."

"It's good to get to know riders from other stables," Allie said. "You might make new friends."

Our waitress came back and took our orders, and I asked for a house burger with mac and cheese on the side.

"I'll have the same," Mila said. "It sounds so good!"

Everyone else ordered, and while we snacked on fresh rolls, Rebecca said, "I'm glad we're having a nice lunch out, because there's something I wanted to discuss with you all."

I stopped chewing to look at her. Everyone's head swiveled in her direction.

"Uh-oh," Nina said.

Rebecca shook her head. "No, it's nothing bad! Sorry, I didn't mean to make you think that."

Whew. For a second, I'd thought we were in trouble!

"You all read *Young Equestrian* magazine, right?" Rebecca asked.

Everyone nodded. Of course we did. It was our Holy Grail magazine!

"Only every single issue," Keir said. "And some back issues too."

That made Rebecca smile. "I've seen so many issues of it lying around the stable that I had a feeling you all enjoyed it."

"It's my go-to magazine," Nina said.

"Well, the editor in chief emailed me this morning," Rebecca said. "Apparently, she's putting together a feature article on up-and-coming young equestrians who have serious potential. Callie said she'd looked into this team, and she's very impressed."

"Wait." I almost couldn't breathe. "Callie Harper, the editor in chief of *YE*, knows about us?"

Callie Harper, one of Sasha's best friends from Canterwood, was a writer who had interviewed Sasha several times for different magazines and websites. She'd competed seriously for a few years before switching to riding for fun and writing equestrian novels and articles. But last year, she'd become *Young Equestrian*'s editor, and she had done some cool articles about other stables and their riding teams. But never one about Foxbury!

Rebecca nodded. "She does. And she wants to fly in from their office in Lexington and do a feature spread on you all. And"—Rebecca grinned—"a cover shoot."

The entire table *erupted*. Everyone was talking at once! I covered my mouth, trying not to shriek in the middle of this restaurant.

"Oh. My. God," Thea said, her cheeks pink. "Are you being serious right now?!"

"Totally serious," Rebecca said. "I didn't email Callie back yet because she asked me to see if you all were even interested first."

"Who wouldn't be interested?!" Selly asked, grinning. "We're in!"

"So very in," I said. "This is wild. We're going to be on the cover of our favorite magazine."

I couldn't even process this. It was almost too much! Every month, I waited for my issue to download onto my iPad so I could read it the second it came in.

"Callie's coming to Foxbury," Keir said slowly. "I can't believe it. It's still rare, you know."

"What is?" Allie asked.

"To meet another Black equestrian," Keir said. "Callie was

one of the first athletes I admired who looked like me. And now, I get to talk to her."

Allie reached over and squeezed Keir's shoulder. "I'm so, so excited for you. That's gonna be wonderful."

The rest of us smiled at Keir. I couldn't wait for him to meet Callie!

"Should I email Callie back?" Rebecca asked. "Or do you all want time to—"

"Email! Email!" Mila said, making Rebecca laugh.

"We don't need time!" I said. "It's a yes!"

"I had a feeling it would be," Rebecca said. "I'll email her after lunch. We'll need to get your parents' permission to be interviewed and photographed for the magazine, of course, but I'm sure they'll all agree. This is a huge opportunity for you, and I was so thrilled to receive an email from Callie."

"When does she want to come?" Thea asked.

"She's not exactly sure about a firm date yet," Rebecca said. "But she mentioned she'd like to get to the interview before the end of the year. So, I'm betting mid-November, or right after Thanksgiving."

That wasn't far off.

The waitress came with our food, and I took a bite of my delicious burger before looking over at Mila.

"We made the right call on what to order," I said. "This is *so* good."

"It really is," she said. "I'm glad I copied you. Wow, can you believe it?" Mila asked me. "We're going to be models!"

"Famous! Models!" I said. "Like, what if other companies see us and want to sponsor us? That would be so exciting."

I'd talked about that before with my friends, and it was something we wanted.

"There are riders our age with sponsorships," she said. "So, fingers crossed."

"Once I have the go-ahead from your parents, we'll get everything set up with Callie," Rebecca said. "And then you all will be tasked with making sure your horses and their belongings are extra neat and clean."

"I've got to go shopping," Selly declared. "None of my clothes are right for a cover."

Thea winced. "Me too. I can't imagine wearing any of my current breeches."

"Hey," Rebecca said firmly, causing us to look at her. "I don't want you stressing over this. It's supposed to be fun! As someone who has seen your riding outfits, trust me, you have plenty of options."

"The magazine already wants you," Allie said. "You don't have to do anything extra besides what you're doing now."

That made me smile. Coming to this adorable, plant-perfect restaurant had been enough. But this news? I couldn't wait to tell Dad!

21

To Us

AFTER A FANTASTIC DINNER, WE ALL got ready in our hotel suites before we rode with Rebecca and Allie to the mixer at Canterwood.

We'd decided not to wear pj's after all and had gone with casual-chic outfits. Selly, however, had dressed to kill in a bright red top and cute black jeans. If she wanted to signal confidence and power going into this party, she'd done that.

As we left the hotel for Canterwood, I sneaked a glance over at Mila for what was surely the twelfth time in the last three minutes. She looked so cute with her hair in a bouncy ponytail.

I wanted to tell her! But we were "friends," and since I'd vowed not to talk to Mila about us until after the show, I probably shouldn't tell her how pretty she looked.

Instead, I gave her a quick smile.

"This party will be fun," Mila said. "Even if no one else talks to us, we'll have each other and the rest of the team."

I nodded. "Yup."

Anxiety made my heart race a little. I wasn't sure if the other riders would be friendly to the Foxbury Four—and the rest of our team was probably guilty by association.

The ride to Canterwood went by way too fast, and before I knew it, I was climbing out of Rebecca's SUV and walking toward Canterwood's ballroom. It was twilight, and early stars winked in the sky as my teammates and I walked with Rebecca and Allie.

"We'll be hanging out and chatting with the other instructors," Rebecca said. "So, feel free to come talk to us if you need anything."

We promised we would and then stepped inside the well-lit ballroom. It was *massive*. There were round tables with beautiful bouquets of sunflowers, orange roses, and calla lilies in the middle of each table. The lighting was soft and warm, and some banquet tables had plenty of snacks, sparkling water, and other beverages. There were groups of riders everywhere, and the adults stood together near the far side of the room, talking and laughing.

"Snacks," I said, my eyes on the treats.

"Let's go," Thea said. She, Mila, and I headed for the trays of food, and as I grabbed a plate, I didn't know what to choose first.

I reached for a pepperoni pizza puff (because, no-brainer) and a spinach cheese ball. I had my eye on a cranberry-and-feta pinwheel too. Ava and Olivia came over to us as I took a bite.

"Ready for tomorrow?" Ava asked.

She and Olivia sipped from their glasses of sparkling water. Even though we were in the same grade, they seemed older than me, with an air of sophistication that I *definitely* didn't have. I felt like the messy younger sister next to them.

"Ready," I said. "Looking forward to getting the first phase going."

"Us too," Ava said.

Ava was well-known in the show circuit as a great dressage rider, so we all had to be on our A games to kick off this competition.

"I'm sure this weekend will be fun too," Olivia said. "We're *bringing it* for the costume contest."

That made me smile. "So are we!"

"I can't wait to see what your costumes are," Thea said.

We chatted for a few more minutes before they wandered off to talk to other people. A few riders side-eyed us and one gave me a dirty look, but no one bothered us, thankfully.

Someone's phone chimed, and Mila pulled hers out of her back pocket. She smiled when she looked at it and tapped out a message before putting down her phone.

"That was Ellie," she said as Emery joined us and met my eye with a knowing glance.

My stomach sank.

"She wanted to wish me luck this weekend!" Mila said.

That was something friends did all the time. So, maybe that was what they were—friends. Still, it made me even more anxious to talk to Mila after the show. What if she and Ellie were really into each other? And Mila was completely over me? It would be the *worst*.

Emery followed me as I wandered away toward the banquet tables, and Thea stayed back with Mila.

"It's going to be okay," Emery whispered. "I bet they're just friends!"

"I guess we'll find out on Sunday when I ask Mila," I said. "Even though I want to talk to her right now and be like, 'Hi, I like you! Please don't date Ellie!'"

"You could," Emery said. "You don't *have* to wait."

I glanced over at Mila, completely torn about what to do. With a sigh, I shook my head. I'd made a plan, and I needed to stick to it. The last thing I needed was for this party to become a disaster.

"I'm going to wait," I said. "But it's sure not easy."

Across the room, Ava and Olivia threw back their heads and laughed at something one of their teammates said. I watched them as they almost glided around the room, talking to different groups of riders. They had the air of girls in charge, but they seemed to rule without Selly's mean streak. I wondered how they did it.

"We can't screw this up tomorrow," Emery said when we got to the drinks table. "Those two will be going hard."

"Yeah, but so will we," I said. "We want to win as badly as they do. Maybe more! We came to Canterwood to prove something. To ourselves and to everyone else who looks at the Foxbury Four and thinks we're . . . *whatever*."

"And I want to prove that I'm a solid member of this team," Emery said. "So, you're right. We're going to put up a fight."

She opened a can of key lime LaCroix and poured some into a glass. I set down my plate and copied her but chose the lemon-flavored option.

Turning to her with a smile, I raised my glass. "To us," I said. "To Foxbury and taking down the competition."

"To us," Emery said, clinking her glass against mine.

I felt more ready to compete than I had in a long time. Our team was going to take down Canterwood!

Team Foxbury

FRIDAY DAWNED COOL AND SUNNY, AND show day one was finally here! My roomies and I slipped into our barn clothes and headed downstairs to the hotel dining room for a continental breakfast.

Selly, Nina, and Keir were already there, loading their plates with waffles, eggs, and fresh fruit. Allie was at a table with a cup of coffee in front of her, reading on her iPad.

I grabbed French toast, bacon, and a glass of OJ. There was an empty table next to the rest of my teammates, so I snagged it and dug in while Thea, Emery, and Mila joined me.

"Dressage day!" Mila said. She took a bite of her bagel-and-egg sandwich. "I'm so ready to go. Hopefully, our inspections will be quick, and we'll have an early call time."

"That would be perfect," I said. "Is it wrong that I kind of want to get dressage out of the way so I can focus on the important thing?"

"The costume contest!" Thea said, grinning.

"The costume contest we're going to *win*," I said.

Someone at the other table snorted, and I didn't have to glance in her direction to know it was Selly.

"We'll see who wins," Selly said.

We finished eating, and I cleared our table just as my phone dinged in my hoodie pocket.

Dad: Good luck today, kiddo! Let me know how it goes! <3

I texted him back.

Abby: Thank youuu! I will! <3

After breakfast, we headed to our suites to gather the clothes we needed for the day. I wasn't changing until the last possible minute, so I wouldn't get dirty.

Then we piled into Rebecca's SUV and made the short drive to Canterwood. The campus was even busier today, since the rest of the riders and their horses had arrived. I spotted Eric giving directions to a group of equestrians, and a dark-haired older man with a stern face pointed out something to some younger riders. He looked extremely no-nonsense.

We walked toward the main barn, and Rebecca stopped us all before we went inside.

"Do you all know what to do?" she asked.

We nodded.

"As team captains, Keir and I are going to the briefing," Thea said. "Then we'll come back and fill everyone in on anything important."

"Good," Rebecca said. "And the rest of you?"

"We'll be grooming our horses and getting them ready for our inspections," I said. "Then we ride!"

Rebecca smiled. "That sounds right to me," she said. "I'll be around to check in, and if you need anything else, you can also ask Allie, Eric, Henry, or Mr. Conner."

Henry Henlein, Canterwood's newest coach, was from Germany, and he worked with Ava and Olivia.

"Got it," Mila said.

"All right, hands in," Rebecca said.

We formed a circle and put our right hands on top of each other.

"Let's get out there and show everyone just how great a team Foxbury is," Rebecca said. "We have some of the most dedicated riders and fantastic horses. Are we ready to win?"

"YES!" we cheered.

"Okay, on three: 'Team Foxbury,'" she said. "One, two . . . three!"

"TEAM FOXBURY!" we yelled, raising our hands in the air.

And with that, we all headed off to grab our horses and get them ready for inspections.

I bent down in front of Beau's tack trunk and frowned. The lid wasn't shut tight. There was no way I'd left it open yesterday, was there?

Maybe you were so tired from getting up early that you didn't close it, I told myself. I lifted the lid up and was hit with a smell so foul and gross it nearly knocked me onto my butt.

Had something *died* in there?!

I put my hand over my mouth and nose, trying not to breathe as I peered in. The entire inside of the trunk—and everything in it—was smeared with something disgusting. I squinted and noticed clumps of scrambled eggs. In the bottom of the trunk, milk—or what I assumed was milk—pooled.

And it smelled like someone had dumped a bottle of vinegar into my trunk to create an eggy, milky, vinegary mess.

I gritted my teeth and stomped over to Circe's stall, where Mila was inside, petting her. "Can you come here a sec?" I asked.

"Sure thing," Mila said, hurrying out and latching the door closed behind her. "What's wrong?"

"Cover your nose," I said, "and look in my trunk."

Hesitantly, Mila peered inside. "No. Way. Did someone egg your trunk? And pour . . . *stuff* in it?"

I nodded, trying not to panic. "This had to have been Selly or Nina. But come *on*, we're all teammates!"

Mila grimaced. "No kidding. Or it was someone else who wanted to try and knock down the competition."

"Maybe," I said, "but my gut says they did it."

I wanted to go track them down and demand to know if they'd done this to me. But then I'd be falling right back into Foxbury Four Abby. And no way was I running to Rebecca about it.

"As much as I want to go talk to Selly and Nina now," I said, "I'm going to clean this up as best I can before inspections. I might need to borrow your non-disgusting grooming kit for Beau once you're finished with it."

"Of course," Mila said. "Use any of my stuff that you want."

The mess was all over my saddle and bridle. My saddle pad was soaked, and there was no time to wash and dry it.

"Did you bring an extra saddle pad?" I asked. "I forgot one. Good job, Abby!"

"I didn't, but I'm sure someone else on our team did," she said. "And don't be hard on yourself. Who expects *this* to happen?"

"Apparently, I should have." Sighing, I lifted my chin and straightened my spine. "Go get Circe ready. I'll come borrow some stuff in a few."

"Okay, and if you need anything, take it," Mila said.

We smiled at each other, and she went back to work.

I took everything out of my tack trunk piece by piece and laid it in the aisle. I grabbed a roll of paper towels off the nearby counter and quickly soaked up all the milk and vinegar at the bottom. It would need to be washed out, but this was all I had time for before my ride. I'd have to clean it all up after, though, so I wouldn't bring down my horse management score.

Beau's grooming kit was a wreck, and paper towels wouldn't

save it. So I set it aside and worked on my saddle and bridle. The smell would probably still be there for a while, but I had to at least get the mess off.

After I got things washed and dried off, I headed for the tack room to borrow some saddle soap. In the hallway, I almost bumped right into Selly.

"What's wrong?" she asked sweetly.

"Nothing," I said. "Everything's great."

"It *is*?" Her brow wrinkled.

I forced a smile. "Yeah! Someone accidentally spilled eggs and milk into my tack trunk, so poor them. But guess what?"

"What?" Selly's eyes widened as she looked at me.

"They did me a favor! It's, like, the best tack cleaner ever! Wait until you see my leather. It's ridiculously shiny!"

"But—" Selly started.

"See you out there," I said, my tone full of cheer.

And before she could say another word, I stepped around her and into the tack room, leaving a very confused Selly behind.

Who knew if I'd win the show, but I'd definitely won that round.

Watch Me

A WHILE LATER, I MOUNTED BEAU, AND we headed for the warm-up arena. Thanks to Mila's grooming kit, I'd gotten him sparkling. And my tack was clean enough for our ride. We'd sailed through our inspection, and now it was time to get ready for our number to be called.

I'm riding at Canterwood Crest Academy, I thought. A grin stretched across my face as I let Beau walk into the arena. This was a space that Sasha, Heather, and Lauren Towers—all famous Canterwood riders—had ridden in. Beau and I weren't at their level yet, but one day we would be. I knew it.

On a loose rein, I let Beau stretch his neck as he walked. I tried to pay attention to him, but all I could do was look around and take this in. But I peered ahead as two riders stopped their horses in my path and stared at me.

Ava and Olivia.

Their mounts looked as polished as they were. Ava's gelding, a rangy chestnut, struck the arena dirt with one front hoof as he eyed Beau. Olivia sat tall on a handsome black gelding with a tiny star on his forehead. He stretched his muzzle forward to touch Beau's and swished his tail while they got to know each other.

"Your horse is sweet," Olivia said.

"Thanks!" I said, smiling. "He's my boy. I'm so glad we're in this together."

Competing without Beau would be an absolute nightmare. I shook off those thoughts and let him meander away from the girls.

We had a class to win!

Beau seemed to feel how focused I was during our warm-up, and he moved easily under me. He responded to every cue and ask of mine, and I felt good going into our turn.

I'd tuned out the other riders being called and concentrated on us.

I brought him down from a slow canter into a collected trot, and my eye caught on a young woman who came over to the rail to watch. Her long, light brown hair hung in pretty waves. She looked stylish in tall boots, a silk scarf tied around her neck, and a light blue button-down shirt like she'd stepped out of a French fashion catalog. There was something familiar about her. I knew her from somewhere. . . .

Oh. My. God.

I almost trotted right into a horse and rider as I craned my neck to sneak another glance at her.

It was Lauren Towers.

Dressage queen Lauren Towers!

Lauren was one of the top United States dressage riders and last year's FEI Dressage world champion in Grand Prix *and* freestyle. She was also going to next year's Pan American Games to compete for our country. A Canterwood Crest grad, Lauren was only a couple of years younger than Sasha.

What was she doing here?

But before I could freak out any more than I already was, the bell sounded, and the loudspeaker crackled to life.

"Number eleven, Abigail St. Clair, please report to arena C for your ride," a voice said. "Again, Abigail St. Clair, number eleven, on Beau of Mine, please head to arena C."

I trotted Beau past Lauren, and she glanced at me, smiling.

"Good luck!" she said.

"Thanks!" I barely got the word out because I was beaming so hard.

Lauren Towers just wished me good luck! But I had to focus, and I could scream about meeting Lauren *after* my ride.

Taking a deep breath, I walked Beau to arena C and quickly glanced at the stands. Allie and Rebecca caught my eye and waved. It felt good to have them both watching and supporting me.

In about five and a half minutes, my ride would be over, and all I'd have to think about for the rest of the day would be the costume contest. And cleaning my trunk.

Focus, I told myself.

It was go time.

I squeezed my legs against Beau's sides and urged him into a working trot. All we had to do was move from letter marker to letter marker in a precise pattern. Absolutely no big deal, except it totally was! We made a straight line right to X, where I halted Beau and saluted the judges.

Back at a working trot, we tracked left to C. I worked hard to keep Beau's trot even and smooth. We flowed through H-X-K before I asked Beau to pick up a working canter on the left lead between A and F.

Keep it together, I thought.

At B, I asked him for a twenty-meter circle to the left. He tossed his head, wanting to make a bigger circle than I allowed. He sidestepped a little, but I got him back on the right track, and we finished our circle neatly.

Beau was an angel through the rein change and working trot, and when we hit A, I slowed him to a nice medium walk.

For a second, I blanked on what was next. Then it came to me. *Free walk from K-X-H.* During our free walk, I let Beau stretch his neck forward and down. He moved so smoothly!

He flowed into a working trot at C, and we headed for the M marker. After we passed it, we started a single loop to X before returning to the track we'd been on just before F.

Beau hit every marker perfectly after F and made a beautiful twenty-meter circle at E. He finished the final moves of the test with clear willingness and eagerness to please. His transitions were calm, and when we headed down the centerline, I had to fight to keep a grin off my face. I kept my gaze focused and between Beau's ears as we came up to X.

I halted him, and he didn't move so much as an ear. We held the position while I saluted, and then I loosened the reins and let him free walk out of the arena.

As I tried not to scream or bounce in the saddle from excitement, I looked over and saw Lauren standing near the rail. She'd watched my entire test, and I hadn't even noticed she was there! *Whew.* If I had, I probably would have messed up!

"Nice test!" she called out to me. "You and your horse make a great team!"

I was going to melt into my saddle. Right now. RIP me.

"Thank you so much!" I said to her.

She smiled at me. "You're welcome!"

I wished I kept a diary or a journal. Because if I did, this moment would sooo be going in there. Like, in all caps and underlined ten times.

Once we were safely out of the arena, I punched the air with my fist, then leaned down and hugged Beau.

"Boy, you were amazing!" I told him. "You did so, so good! I'm proud of you!"

Beau snorted, flexing his neck. He pranced forward, and I laughed, letting him party a little.

"I bet you'll be excited to get turned out with your friends tonight," I said. "You'll get to tell them all how you rocked your test."

I dismounted and loosened his girth. He was pretty cool, but I wanted to walk him for a few minutes to make sure. Plus, I needed him to feel good for later!

Before we headed to cool out, I glanced up at the scoreboard and waited to see our test score.

Then it flashed onto the screen.

ST. CLAIR, ABIGAIL: 70.00 (30.00)

"YES, BOY!" I said to Beau. I hugged his neck, squeezing him tight. "That's a great score for us!"

The first number was our test score, and the second was our penalty points.

We had done our part for today. We'd been the first on our team to go, and I trusted the rest of my teammates to do well.

"Now it's time to walk and get you cool," I told him.

As we headed for his cooldown, I couldn't help but feel proud of us for our ride. And once Beau was safely back in his stall, I was going to clean up my tack trunk and wash away the last remnants of Selly's prank. She had tried to hit back at me for messing up her show last year, and she had failed.

Miserably.

Costumed Cuties

STILL FULL FROM DINNER, THEA AND I
were in the upstairs loft of our hotel suite, getting
ready for the costume contest. Emery and Mila were
downstairs, doing hair and makeup. I still had no idea what
their costumes were, and they'd wanted to keep them a surprise until it was time to leave.

Foxbury had closed out the day with *excellent* marks in
dressage. I was in first place individually, and my team was
in first too, with Canterwood's team in second, and Keir's
team in third. We'd all walked the cross-country course

before leaving for the hotel, and I felt good about it.

Now I was completely focused on my costume. I was going as the Headless Horseman, and Thea was Ichabod Crane. We were going to have the best costumes *ever*!

"I still can't believe Selly did that to you," Thea said, shaking her head. She was slicking her hair back into a low bun to try to look more like the schoolteacher.

"I probably should have told Rebecca, but I've kind of had enough drama already this year," I said. "It made me nervous to even think about telling her."

"Abs, she wouldn't have been mad at you," Thea said. "You didn't do anything wrong. Selly did."

I shrugged. "I know. But I didn't want her to think I'm always a problem. Always the drama. This was something I could handle myself, and I did."

"As your friend, I'm still annoyed. But as your team captain, I'm really thankful for how you handled it," Thea said. "The easy thing would have been to blow up at her, but you didn't."

"Hopefully, she feels all warm and fuzzy now and like she's gotten her revenge on me," I said. "Then we can put that entire mess behind us and move on."

"I hope so too."

We went back to getting ready. I pulled my hair into a bun so I could fit my fake-bloodied neck cap on. The last parts of my costume were a plastic sword and a creepy jack-o'-lantern to throw at Ichabod. Thankfully, Dad's credit card had allowed me to purchase both items, and I'd brought them with me.

Thea put on her jaunty hat and caught my eye. "Well," she asked, "do I look like a teacher who falls in love with the fair maiden, Katrina? Then gets murdered by the Headless Horseman?"

I tapped my chin with my index finger, pretending to think. "Hmmm," I said. "Yes, I think you do. I look forward to throwing a flaming pumpkin at you later."

We giggled.

"And by flaming, I mean a flameless battery-operated candle inside the jack-o'-lantern," I said.

"Don't ruin the illusion," Thea said, groaning.

We tugged on our boots and crowded together for a selfie. I posted the pic on Instagram with the caption, *Happy Halloween from Ichabod and the Headless Horseperson!*

"We're coming down!" I called down the stairs to Emery

and Mila. Honestly, I couldn't wait another minute to see their costumes.

I hurried down to the bathroom. The door was open, and Mila and Emery were inside.

Mila turned around, and I felt my jaw drop in the most ridiculous and clichéd way ever.

"*Whoa,*" I said. "You're Poison Ivy!"

Mila grinned, and when she blinked, I noticed the glittery green eye shadow on her lids. Her red hair was loose and curled into soft waves. She'd put on a shamrock-colored tutu with a matching bodysuit that had ivy climbing all over it. Green tights and black riding boots pulled the whole look together.

"And Circe is Harley Quinn!" she said. "I got the cutest stuff for her to wear."

"I love it!" I said.

Then I dragged my eyes away from Mila to look at Emery.

"Oh my god, Em!" I said, clutching my hands together in front of me. "You look *awesome*!"

And she did! Emery had completely transformed into Sally from *The Nightmare Before Christmas*. She'd done the makeup perfectly and even had on Sally's raggedy dress.

"Please tell me Bliss is Zero," I said.

Emery nodded. "Bliss is totally Zero. I can't wait to do her makeup!"

"This is the best Halloween ever!" I said. "Wait till you see Thea! Foxbury has this costume contest on *lock*."

"You two look so good!" Thea squealed and came up behind me.

"So do you!" Mila said. "Abby, you look so creepy! And Thea, you're a great Ichabod!"

That made Thea and me grin.

"Ready to go?" I asked everyone.

My friends nodded.

"Let's take a group pic first," I said.

In the living room area, we smooshed together and mugged for the camera. After I got a few pics, it was time to go!

We headed for the elevator to meet Rebecca in the lobby.

"Canterwood isn't ready for us," Thea said.

I grinned. "No, they definitely aren't!"

At Canterwood, the entire place had been transformed almost as if by Halloween goblins. And the full moon that was out only added to the eeriness! The once-bare arena C's rails were now wrapped with orange-and-black ribbon, there were stacks of pumpkins scattered around, and a scarecrow watched over everything from up in the stands.

Costumed riders were everywhere! There were lots of superheroes and anime characters. And a couple of zombies and princesses.

In the stable, Mila and Emery headed off to get their horses done up. I turned to Thea and wiggled my eyebrows.

"Want to get Beau and Chaos ready together, since we're partners?" I asked.

"Absolutely," she said. "I think Ichabod's stallion was a plow horse, so he wasn't very fancy or done up, but I want to paint Chaos's hooves with some silver glitter. And do his tail and mane."

"It *is* Halloween," I said. "I want to do the same to Beau, but with red. And when I put my cape on, it's long enough that I can drape it over Beau's hindquarters. It's gonna look so good!"

We led our horses out of their stalls and clipped them into nearby crossties. Beau was already clean from when I'd groomed him post-dressage, and so was Chaos.

I dug around in my clean tack trunk for some clear

rubber bands to use in Beau's mane and tail. Beau dozed while I braided, and I wove ruby-red ribbons into some of his mane braids. They gave a dramatic effect to his look.

Then I found my bottle of red Twinkle Toes glitter hoof polish, and I painted Beau's hooves. It complemented the red in his mane, and I loved the sparkle!

Once we got the horses ready, we stood them next to each other for pics.

"They look sooo good!" Thea said.

I nodded. "And so do we!"

Thea glanced at her phone. "We can head to the arena now. The judging will begin soon."

I grabbed my neck cap, sword, cape, and plastic pumpkin. "I'm going to need your help," I said, laughing. "There's a lot happening here."

"Of course," Thea said. "Go ahead and mount, and then I'll hand you stuff."

It took a few minutes for me to get settled on Beau with the other pieces of my costume in place. But once I was set, Thea stepped back and grinned at me. I could see her through the black mesh of my stand-up collar that wrapped around my head.

"You look *terrifying*," she said. "I'm a little afraid of you, and I know who you are under all of that!"

I did my best evil laugh. "Excellent. Let's go!"

Thea climbed up on Chaos's back, and together we headed into the arena.

"Wow," I said. "People did *not* mess around with their costumes!"

Thea shook her head. "They sure didn't!"

My eyes didn't know where to look. Keir and Magic were walking around—Keir had dressed as a knight, and Magic was his trusty jousting steed. Nina was an annoyingly adorable sheepherder, and she'd covered Adore in giant cotton balls and given him horns to make him look like a sheep.

"Move, losers."

Thea and I glanced behind us as Selly urged Ember around us and forward toward the rail. Selly had transformed into Belle, complete with a gorgeous yellow gown and beautiful updo. She'd put a furry brown fly mask with horns on Ember to turn the mare into the Beast. She'd even added matching furry leg wraps, and a blue blanket with gold trim that she'd made to look like a coat.

"Be nice, princess," Thea called after her.

"Not a chance, Ichabod!" Selly said back.

Mila entered the arena and headed over to Thea and me.

"Circe looks so good!" I said. "I love her costume!"

The mare looked supercute in a blond wig with pink and blue pigtails, a red-and-black blanket made to look like a T-shirt, and a baseball bat that Mila had attached near her withers.

"Thank you," Mila said, smiling. "She's being very well-behaved despite the wig. I'm shocked."

Usually, Circe was as hot as Chaos, but the two horses seemed to enjoy the fun atmosphere.

"Maybe she knows this is a costume contest and not a lesson or a show," I said, "so she can relax."

Mila nodded. "Probably. And dang, you and Thea are the best pair by far!" She looked at me with wide eyes. "You're creeping me out a little, Abs."

I thrust my sword into the air. "My plan is working!"

Thea and Mila laughed.

But the laughter died down when Ava and Olivia rode their horses into the arena. In fact, it felt as though every pair of eyes in here turned to look at them.

"Holy—" I started.

"Crap," Thea finished.

Ava and Olivia were in stunning pastel dresses with long white-blond wigs. They sat sidesaddle on their horses, who had been painted head to hoof to look like blue and green dragons. Their coats had intricate, varied scales that shimmered when caught in a certain light. On each of their laps rested a dragon egg. Both of them sported twin smug smirks. Whoa. I'd only seen clips of that show, since Dad said it was too old me for me.

"Honestly, I'd be smirking too," I whispered to Thea and Mila. "If I showed up looking like that? Automatic right to smirk all day."

"Agreed," Thea said.

"They're gonna be tough to beat," I said.

We lined up for Eric, Mr. Conner, and the other instructor, who I assumed was Henry.

The judges started at the far end of the line and worked their way down toward Thea, Mila, and me. As they strolled, they pointed out different things they liked about each costume and marked notes on their clipboards.

"And this is Abby from Foxbury," Eric said to his fellow coaches when he reached me. I smiled, happy he'd remembered my name. "She and her friend, Thea, are a pairs costume."

"Your outfit, minus the prosthetic, is something I'd wear to teach lessons," Mr. Conner said, winking at me.

I laughed. "You're welcome to borrow the cape!"

"I just might take you up on that," he said.

"And have Mr. Conner be even more intimidating to students than he already is?" Eric joked. "No way!"

They talked to Thea and Mila, complimenting their costumes too. Then they headed back toward the center of the arena for one last look and to choose a winner.

I crossed my fingers for anyone from Foxbury. As long as it wasn't Ava or Olivia, I'd be good with the decision.

"Thank you all for showing us your fantastic creativity!" Mr. Conner said, smiling at us. "It wasn't an easy verdict to reach, but I think we've made our choices."

He glanced at Eric and Henry, who nodded.

"The winner is Selly from Foxbury!" Mr. Conner said. He, Eric, and Henry clapped, and the rest of us broke into applause.

"Second place goes to Ava and Olivia from Canterwood Crest," Eric said.

"And our third-place winners are Abby and Thea from Foxbury!" Henry said.

"Yessss!" I cheered.

"Yay!" Thea let out a whoop and reached over to give me a high five.

"We have Halloween-themed gift baskets for all of you," Mr. Conner said. "Everyone should feel proud of what they did, and we can't wait to see what you all do next year."

Basking in the glow of third place, I headed Beau to the rail for a victory lap in our costumes!

Let's Go!

THE NEXT DAY, I WAS BACK AT THE stable bright and early for cross-country. It was overcast, but there wasn't rain in the forecast, and I was grateful that we wouldn't be taking the horses out on a muddy course. I also wasn't mad about the gray weather—it made everything feel eerie and much more like Halloween.

"How're you feeling?" I asked Mila. She and I had completed our safety check together and were waiting near the start box. I was riding next, and she was after me.

"Nervous but okay," she said. "I'm trying to remind myself

that it's a fun course, and the jumps are so cool! Hopefully, that will make me less anxious."

"You're going to do great," I said. "Stay focused on Circe and think about your ride."

That made her smile. "Thanks, Abs."

Beau snorted, tugging the reins through my fingers. He was ready to go after his warm-up!

"Hey, wait your turn," I said to him. "We'll get our signal to start in a minute."

Beside us, Circe crab-stepped away from Beau. Mila patted the mare's neck and cooed to her. Then she looked over at me. "I'm going to walk her for a bit. I'll be sending you all the good vibes!"

"Okay," I said. "See you on the other side!"

We traded smiles, and she headed off.

"Abigail St. Clair on Beau of Mine from Foxbury, please enter the starting box," someone said over the loudspeaker.

"We've got this, boy," I said.

Beau moved fluidly under me as he walked toward the start box. I couldn't wait to get out there, and I knew Beau felt the same way!

We entered the box, and I took a deep breath. Seven

obstacles were between us and the end. I sank my weight into my tailbone and sat still, waiting for the starting bell.

Ding!

At the bell, I turned Beau toward the exit of the box and let him out at a trot. Once we were a few strides away from the box, I gave him rein, and he moved into a smooth canter. We cantered over the grass, and I spotted the first obstacle up ahead.

It was a line of black cauldrons with purple lights inside of them that glowed out of the top, and orange rails on either side.

Beau pricked both ears forward and cantered up to the jump. At the right second, I lifted my butt out of the saddle and slid my hands along Beau's neck. He lifted into the air, not even glancing at the could-be-scary cauldrons and their lights. He landed easily on the other side, and we cantered to the next jump.

I looked ahead toward the feed trough filled with tiny plastic pumpkins and gourds. Beau didn't look twice at it, and he sailed over the obstacle.

"Good boy," I told him.

I let him gain a bit of speed as we started up a slight hill. Beau snorted, tossing his head, and charged up and over the hill. We came down the other side, and once we hit the flat ground, I collected him. Beau cantered along for a couple of minutes before we reached the third jump. This one was giant logs painted white with black ghost faces.

I clicked to Beau and got him to speed up as we approached the logs.

Three, two, one . . . now!

On *now*, I moved into the two-point position as Beau rocked back on his haunches and arched over the jump. I couldn't help but grin. This was the best feeling in the world. I wished I could freeze us, suspended in the air, and stay there for as long as possible. But Beau landed cleanly on the other side, and I praised him.

The next jump could be tricky. I knew what Beau liked and didn't like, and I had a feeling this one could get his attention. And not in a good way.

So I kept my legs on him and urged him forward with my hands and seat as he cantered along the grass.

We made a long, smooth turn, and the fourth obstacle came into view. This jump had bright orange, purple, and yellow flames painted onto a flat sheet of wood. Purple streamers were attached to either end of the jump, and I had to hope there wouldn't be a sudden breeze that would cause them to whip around in the air.

My eye caught on one of the many officials who were stationed along every jump to watch us. For a moment, I wondered if they'd witnessed horses spook at this jump. Or if everyone had made it over safely.

For once, I hadn't looked up the current standings of the other riders before my ride, and because of where my turn fell, I hadn't seen any of my teammates who had ridden yet.

Focus, Abby, focus.

But as we approached the fake flames, it was like the devil himself came to play for Halloween. A stiff breeze kicked up, and the streamers on the jump twisted and flapped in the wind.

Beau popped his head and snorted, and I sat deeper in the saddle and used my seat to let him know that running out or stopping wasn't an option. We were going over the flames. No matter what.

But Beau wobbled beneath me, his stride slowing. I tapped him with my heels, then squeezed my legs against his sides.

"C'mon," I said, my voice firm. "You can do it!"

I urged him forward with my hands and seat and got him back up to a decent speed. Beau jumped high, high, *high* into the air, clearing the wooden flames and the scary streamers.

There was an extra bounce in his step after he landed and cantered a few strides away. He was *totally* saying, *Take that!*

"Yay, boy!" I said. "Three more!"

We hit a stretch of grass that was perfect for galloping. I let Beau move into a slow gallop as he flew over the ground with smooth strides.

This. Was. Perfection.

I loved everything about this! I couldn't ask for a better horse than Beau, and it was such a fun course. Once Mila got out here, she'd feel it too, and I knew she and Circe would have no problem.

Wind whipped in my ears as I eased Beau to a steady canter. He felt strong and energized beneath me as I pointed him toward the fifth jump—a row of pumpkins stacked three and four high and four deep. Beau hopped over them without a second glance, and we made our way toward the ditch.

This one could be tricky too. It wasn't a typical ditch jump. Instead, it had a life-sized skeleton at each end, and there was a pile of skeletons in the ditch. The skeletons would totally cause Beau to eyeball the obstacle. But hopefully, I'd keep him moving.

As the skeletons came into closer view, I felt Beau thinking hard as he tried to work out in his head what those creepy white bony things were. I fought to channel every bit of confidence I had into him, reassuring him we could do this.

It must have worked, because Beau kept up his speed and didn't slow. At the correct distance, he rocked back on his haunches and launched himself over the ditch, skeletons and all.

Maybe he loved Halloween as much as I did! He was taking everything in stride and wasn't too afraid of the haunted decor.

"One more, boy!"

I didn't need to glance at my watch to know we were making great time. But still, I let Beau move into a fast canter as we headed around a turn and made our way to the final jump.

This one, stacked hay bales with a giant witch standing at each end, wouldn't faze Beau. A witch wasn't that scary!

"Let's go!" I told him. "We're almost done!"

He cantered right up to the jump, eager and willing, and he soared into the air at precisely the right second.

He hit the ground well away from the bales, hooves thundering on the grass. I shoved my hands along his neck and asked him to give it everything he had to carry us over the finish line.

And boy, did he! Beau flattened into a ground-eating gallop and powered through to the end, where Rebecca was waiting.

"YES, ABBY!" Rebecca yelled.

I let out a whoop and slowed Beau to a canter and then a trot. After a few strides, I slowed him to a walk and then halted him to hop off and loosen his girth.

"He was so good!" I told Rebecca as she came over to us.

"And no time faults!" she cheered.

"Yay! I didn't think we'd have any based on how he was going. But I *have* been caught off guard before."

Rebecca was next to me as I walked Beau toward the vet box.

"I'm really proud of that ride," Rebecca said. "Beau started to waver a couple of times, but I saw you keep him moving and not let up on him. You made sure he knew he was going over those obstacles."

I smiled at the compliment. "Thank you. I didn't want to bully him over them, but I wanted him to know that I wouldn't be happy if he tried to refuse."

Rebecca slung her arm over my shoulders and squeezed. "You did great. Our team is lucky to have you."

And as I led Beau into the vet box for his post-cross-country check, I replayed Rebecca's words in my head over and over while I waited for Mila and Circe to join us.

An Invitation

A SHORT WHILE LATER, A GRINNING Mila led Circe into the vet box. Her red pony-tail swished as she walked, and Circe held her head proudly.

"You crushed it?" I asked, already knowing the answer based on her face.

"We crushed it!" Mila confirmed. "Those good vibes you sent us must have been magical, because Circe was so perfect! She listened to me at every jump, and I don't think there was a single second where I was worried."

"Yaaaay!" I hugged her, wondering how she smelled like vanilla after being around horses all day. Was she some kind of adorable witch?! "I'm so happy for you. I knew you'd have a great ride. I could feel it."

"Thank you! But enough about me," she said. "How did you do? Tell me everything!"

"We nailed it too," I said. "It's like the Canterwood gods were smiling down on us. Beau had a couple of moments where he thought about not doing what I asked, but we worked it out. We had a great run!"

"Now we just have to hope that Thea and Nina kill it."

"I hope they do," I said. "I haven't looked at any standings from cross-country, but I will once I get Beau back to the stable."

Mila nodded. "I haven't either. I didn't want to psych myself out if everyone before me had perfect rides or make myself worry about the course if there were lots of runouts and refusals."

"Understandable," I said. "I'm going to go groom Beau. But I'll meet you in the stable?"

"Definitely. We'll be there in a few."

I led Beau away from the vet box, patting his neck. "You

were an absolute dream. I'm so proud of you, and thank you for two amazing phases."

It meant the world to me to come here and do our very best.

"You'll be getting lots of carrots later," I told Beau. "And! After you're groomed, we're gonna turn you out. You can graze and kick up your heels with your friends."

Beau bobbed his head.

In the stable, I took off Beau's slightly sweaty tack, haltered him, and clipped him into crossties. I always tried to take my time grooming him after a class. It was important to me to make him feel as good as possible and know that at the end of competing, he got a good reward.

But first, I pulled out my phone and checked the current results. I was still hanging on to first place! Canterwood's team was right on our tail, though, so we couldn't afford a single mistake.

I grabbed Beau's rubber curry comb from his tack box and worked it in small circles to loosen up the sweat-dried patches of hair on his coat. Then I ducked into a nearby bathroom and quickly put a few inches of warm water into a bucket. Beau needed a little sponge bath to wipe away the crud.

Once I got him clean, I rubbed him with a towel. He

loved every second of it. His ears flicked back and forth, and his tail occasionally swished gently as he napped.

"You're definitely getting a spa day once we get home," I said. "Massage, mane and tail, hooves—all of it."

I lost myself in caring for him and only looked up from combing his tail when someone cleared their throat.

"Hey," I said, looking up at Ava and Olivia.

"What are you doing tonight?" Ava asked.

Umm, *what?*

"Nothing?" I had no idea why she was asking me this. "Well, probably ordering takeout with my roommates and watching TV."

"That sounds . . . fine," Ava said. She shrugged one shoulder.

"What about you?" I asked. "Is there something around here I should do instead of hanging in the hotel?"

They traded glances and then nodded.

"We want you to meet us at Walnut Park tonight," Ava said. "You, Selly, Nina, and Thea."

The Foxbury Four.

And I'd seen plenty of riders taking lunches to Walnut Park. It was on the edge of Canterwood's campus and within walking distance of the hotel.

Still, there was no way I'd agree to this, but I'd let them think I wanted to find out more about what was going on.

"Why?" I asked. "I have to tell my coach something if I want to go somewhere."

Ava shook her head, her silky dark blond hair flying. "No, this is between us." She grinned. "Unless you're scared."

"I'm not—" I stopped, taking a breath. "I'm not scared."

But I was! If I left the hotel and got caught? Rebecca would have a coronary. She'd throw me off the riding team so fast, my head would spin.

The air was charged among us, and my curiosity started to get to me. I'd never snuck out before! It sounded a little dangerous and a lot exciting. I stared at them and shook my head. "Why do you want to meet us? At night? And in *secret*?"

They gave me angelic smiles.

"Tell me why you want to meet," I said.

But instead of answering, they wiggled their fingers at me.

"See you tonight! Eight o'clock," Ava said. "Or not!"

And then they were gone.

I looked at Beau, wide-eyed. "I . . . have no idea what *that* was," I said. "Do you?"

Beau blinked sleepily at me.

"Sneaking out to meet them would be the worst idea ever," I whispered to Beau. "But maybe they're making an effort to be friendly! Turning them down would be rude, right?"

I winced, knowing I needed to talk to Selly, Nina, and Thea, but not until after today's comp had ended. I'd learned my lesson there, that was for sure.

With a sigh, I went back to grooming Beau. There was nothing I could do until I talked to my teammates, anyway.

Later, when we were all at the hotel, I started a group text to Thea, Selly, and Nina. Thea was over in Keir's room, talking to him about team captain stuff. I hadn't told her anything about my conversation with Ava and Olivia, mainly because I knew she'd have *lots* of questions and it would be easier to answer them all at once with everyone there.

Abby: Hey, can you all meet me in the hotel lobby in 5?

Selly: Why?

Abby: Please? It's about Ava and Olivia.

Thea: Yeah, of course. See you in 5.

Then I got a text just to me from Thea.

Thea: What's going on??

Quickly, I wrote her back.

Abby: I'll tell you in a min!

Emery and Mila were under blankets on the couch, watching an old nineties rom-com. They were quickly becoming friends, and it made me glad that they got along.

I slipped out of the room and headed downstairs to the lobby.

Selly, Nina, and Thea were already waiting.

"This better be good," Selly said.

Together, we went over to an empty seating area and sat down. There was a gorgeous fish tank near us, and I had to work to tear my eyes away from the colorful fish and focus on my teammates.

"Sooo, Ava and Olivia were chatty with me earlier," I said. "And they wanted to know if we had plans tonight."

Selly, Nina, and Thea couldn't have looked more confused.

"They want to hang out with *us*?" Thea asked, wrinkling her brow. "Why?"

Quickly, I filled them in.

"Well, they're just going to have to think we're afraid of getting caught," Thea said, "because there's a *zero* percent chance I'm sneaking out of the hotel to meet them." Her gaze was firm as she looked at us. "Zero."

"That's how I felt," I said.

Thea whipped her head around to look at me. "'Felt'?"

"Well, I thought about it, and I don't know, but I kind of want to go," I said.

"Abby!" Thea's mouth fell open. "You're joking. Come on. You know better."

A smile curled onto Selly's glossy pink lips. "Leave her alone, Thea. Maybe Abby's in the mood for a little fun. An adventure."

Thea glanced at Nina. "And you?"

Nina took a deep breath and chewed on her bottom lip. "If we go, we stick together. We hear what they have to say, and then we come back here. No one will find out."

"But what if Rebecca does?" Thea asked. "If we get caught, we're kicked off the team. You all know this. There's no coming back for a third chance if she finds out."

"Then we better not get caught," Selly said.

Surprise!

FTER DINNER, I SAT WITH EMERY and Mila in our suite and explained to them what had happened with Ava and Olivia. I didn't want to just disappear into the night without an explanation. Thea was already downstairs, walking off her anxiety about going.

"Abby, this is a *bad* idea," Emery said. "You're going to get caught! Or what if this is some kind of trick?"

Mila nodded. "Yeah, why else would they try to get you to leave the hotel and come to Canterwood? All they have to do is spill that you're there, and bam—you're off the team."

"That's what I thought at first too," I said. "But if they're meeting us, too? They could get busted for going out after hours without permission."

Emery shook her head slowly. "But they're also not on thin ice with their instructor, are they? Meaning, they might have one more chance. You don't. You, Selly, Nina, and Thea are out of chances."

"Yeah . . . ," Mila said. "If you get caught, you're *done*."

Nerves made my stomach feel a little bubbly and unsettled. "I know. I do. But I want to go. Even though I shouldn't! But I won't get caught. Canterwood's minutes away from here. We'll go, see what they want, and come right back."

"What if Rebecca notices the four of you are missing?" Emery asked, chewing on her thumbnail.

"This hotel is huge," I said. "We could be at the pool, the vending machines, working out—there are so many options!"

"True," Emery said.

"If Rebecca asks us where you are?" Mila asked.

"Then tell her the truth," I said firmly. "There's no reason for you to get in trouble covering for us."

Emery and Mila glanced at each other before looking back at me.

"Not gonna lie, I'd probably go too," Mila said. "I'm dying to know what they want to talk about."

"Me too," Emery said.

I smiled. "I'm sorry you weren't invited to this potentially catastrophic event. I'll make sure to tell them you're coming next time."

We all laughed, and I checked the time.

"I better head down to the lobby to meet Thea, Selly, and Nina," I said.

"Good luck," Mila said, her eyes wide with worry. "You better come back still a member of this team!"

"I will," I said. "Promise."

Emery wished me good luck too, and I left our room, shutting the door gently behind me. Rebecca and Allie were such early risers that they were possibly already asleep. They hadn't come to check on us at night before, so it didn't seem likely that they would now.

On the elevator ride down, I wondered again if this was a good idea. It probably—no, it *definitely* wasn't. But I wasn't going to back out now.

In the lobby, I found Selly, Nina, and Thea already huddled together. They glanced up with guilty expressions on their faces until they saw it was me, and then they slumped forward a little.

"There are my girls! Well, some of them."

I gasped a little and whirled around to face Rebecca, who had an ice bucket under one arm. She eyed us, and I was sure she could see the anxiety on our faces.

"Hiii!" I said, my voice squeaky. "What're you doing?"

Sigh, Abby.

Rebecca held up the ice bucket. "Getting ice. What about you four?"

"Um." I shot a panicked look at Thea.

"Working out," she answered quickly.

"Yeah!" I said. "Going swimming."

I wanted to smack myself in the face.

"In those clothes?" Rebecca raised an eyebrow.

Selly shot me a dirty look. I was the *worst* at this!

"She means swimming *after* we work out," Selly said smoothly. "Right, Abby?"

"Right," I said weakly. "After, of course."

And because things had to get worse, Keir came out of the elevator and walked toward us, a cheery smile on his face. "Hey! What's everyone doing?"

"Working out!" Nina said. "We're heading to the gym now, so we better go."

Keir frowned and checked his phone. "Aren't the gym and pool closed now?"

The four of us shot him a *shut up!* look, but he was completely oblivious to it. Sweat prickled under my arms, and I considered forgetting this whole thing.

"Well," Selly said brightly. "We'll do laps inside the hotel, then. So many stairs and hallways!" She motioned for us to follow her. "C'mon!"

And before Keir could offer to tag along, the four of us darted away and headed for the stairwell.

"Don't forget lights out at nine thirty!" Rebecca called after us. "We have a big day tomorrow!"

Once the door had closed behind us, we burst into laughter.

"Now what?" I asked. "Rebecca could be chilling in the lobby!"

Nina sighed. "With her ice? Don't think so."

"Let's wait five minutes, then go," Selly said. "She'll be back in her room by then."

So we waited, watching the time on my phone.

"Ready?" I asked, my mouth dry.

Thea, Selly, and Nina nodded. Selly eyed me and snorted.

"What?" I asked.

"Did you really change into all black for this?" she asked.

I frowned. "Yeah? We're sneaking!"

Unlike me, the other three were wearing clothes with bright colors.

Selly rubbed her forehead and sighed. "Exactly. We're sneaking, not *burglarizing*!"

"Well, okay, Miss Expert," I said.

Selly laughed. Even Nina cracked a smile.

We left the stairwell and headed back into the lobby. I turned and headed toward the front doors, yelping a bit as someone tugged on the back of my sweater.

"Abby!" Selly hissed. "We're not going out the *front* door!"

"Act like you've at least done some sneaking before!" Nina said, rolling her eyes.

I followed them down the hallway, and giggling, we went out the back door of the hotel. It was dark out now, but the parking lot was lit up by streetlights.

"We did it, oh my god," I said.

Selly looked at me with an amused expression. "This is . . . the parking lot," she said. "We haven't done anything yet."

"I think Rebecca would disagree with that," Thea said.

This felt dangerous! And fun! I'd been so nervous to do it, but now that I was out of the hotel, my heart raced, and I felt *alive*.

"Is this how it starts?" I asked Selly.

She wrinkled her nose. "How what starts?"

"A life of bad behavior," I said. "Like, first you sneak out. Next thing you know, you're staying out all night!"

Selly looked like she wanted to pat me on the head. "St. Clair, I can assure you, there's a zero percent chance this will be your gateway into a world of bad behavior."

Unconvinced, I eyed her. She and Nina probably snuck out all the time, and this was no big deal to them. But this was the first time I'd ever gone anywhere without permission, and hopefully, it wouldn't end with me getting caught.

The walk to Walnut Park didn't take long. The sidewalk was well lit, and I recognized a few riders from the hotel hanging out and talking. But seeing them made me extra nervous. What if someone told Rebecca they'd seen us here?

"Thought you weren't coming," a smirking Ava said as we walked up to her and Olivia. They were seated inside an adorable gazebo all lit up with twinkly lights.

"We were bored," Nina said.

My hands shook a little, but I tried to remind myself that every kid in the history of time had snuck out before. I had to stay calm and try to have fun. It was too late to go back now.

It felt so weird to be on campus at night. I was half expecting Rebecca to be here, secretly alerted by Ava and Olivia and ready to yell at us for sneaking out. But there was no Rebecca.

"So. A gazebo?" Selly asked. She jutted out one hip. "We have these at home."

"This is where we feel safe to talk," Olivia said. "People can be weird and, you know, record stuff."

Yeah, did I ever.

Ava shrugged. "It can wind up online. We like privacy."

"Listen, none of us are recording you, because we don't care that much," Selly said. "So, please tell us whatever it is you want to say so we can get back to our hotel."

"Selly, chill," Ava said. "We asked you four here because, despite everything you've done, we like you."

"Why?" I asked, confused.

"We're the queens of Canterwood," Ava said simply. "And you four run Foxbury."

"Well, we *were* the queens of Canterwood," Olivia said.

"'Were'?" Thea asked.

Ava and Olivia smiled, their teeth gleaming in the street-light. Goose bumps prickled my arms.

"Surprise!" Ava said. "We're transferring to Foxbury *and* Saddlehill!"

Allies or Enemies?

THE SOUNDS OF THE PARK FELL AWAY. All I could hear was my loud breathing as I stared at Ava and Olivia.

"What?" I asked.

"You're *what?*" Nina asked.

Beside me, Selly swallowed so hard, I saw her throat bob up and down.

"Why?" Thea asked. "Don't you bleed gold and green?"

Those were Canterwood's colors.

"Yeah, isn't your school the *best?*" Nina asked.

This could not be real. They had to be pranking us.

Ava and Olivia shrugged.

"Let's just say we're a little tired of this place," Ava said.

"That can't be true," I said, trying to keep my tone light. "C'mon, what's the real reason?"

"That's the only reason you're getting," Olivia said coolly.

I swallowed, forcing myself not to take a step back.

"Why bring us here to tell us this?" Selly asked. "You could have told us all this tomorrow. Or, you know, over social media or something."

Olivia snorted. "Where's the fun in that?"

"We wanted to tell you in person because who knows what we could do together once we're teamed up at Foxbury," Ava said.

"We worked *very* hard at Canterwood to be at the top," Olivia added. "We're looking forward to doing the same at Foxbury. With you."

No. They couldn't be serious! They were going to be great additions to our show teams, sure, but competing against them to be at the top at my stable was going to be *brutal*.

"Look, you both seem cool, but coming to Foxbury and Saddlehill is weird," Selly said.

For once, I was glad she was around. She said exactly what we all had to be thinking!

"What's weird about transferring?" Ava asked.

"There's no way you would leave Canterwood," Selly said, "especially as the so-called queens. There's a reason you're leaving. And there's a motive for coming to Foxbury."

"Ooh," Olivia said, smiling. "You make it sound like a fun mystery game."

"It's not a game," Nina said sharply. "This is our team. We've worked hard to get where we are, and if you're joining us, I hope you're coming to be good teammates."

"We are," Ava said. She locked eyes with Nina. "We promise."

I didn't know what to think. This was all too much, too fast. Something in my gut told me that Selly was right and these two had a serious reason for wanting to transfer. But judging by the way Ava and Olivia were acting, they weren't going to tell us, which meant we were wasting our time standing around here talking to them.

"We should go," I said. "We don't want anyone to notice we're missing. Or spot us here."

"Of course," Olivia said. "Thanks for meeting us. We're going to be the best team, I can tell."

"See you tomorrow!" Ava said, smiling. "Can't wait for us to be official teammates soon!"

"Yeah," I said weakly. "Can't wait."

The four of us turned away and walked quickly back down the sidewalk. Selly looked shaken, and I couldn't help but wonder if she was worried about her spot at Foxbury. She was *our* team's self-appointed queen, and when these two powerful riders joined? It would be a fight for the throne.

While we walked, my phone buzzed in my hand. I almost dropped it, half-convinced it was Ava and Olivia, having somehow gotten my number.

I glanced at the screen as more texts kept appearing.

Emery: YOU BETTER GET HERE FAST!!!

Emery: ABBY!!!

Emery: Rebecca's visiting our room to strategize for tomorrow!! She wants everyone there

Mila: ABBY HURRY UP REBECCA IS COMING

"Oh my god," I said. "C'mon! That was Emery and Mila!"

My teammates and I broke into a run, dashing away from Walnut Park.

"What's wrong?!" Thea asked.

"They said Rebecca's coming to talk about tomorrow!"
I said.

Selly's face was ghostly pale under the streetlamps.

Quickly, I texted them back.

Abby: We're on our way!!

Anxiety gnawed at my stomach, and I thought I was going
to barf.

"It's going to be fine," Selly said, even though her voice
shook. "We'll sneak back into the hotel and go to the vending machines first. Then we can tell Rebecca we were walking
around and grabbing snacks."

"That's a good idea," Thea said. "And then it's not a lie—
we really were there."

I swallowed. "Unless Mila and Emery tell her the truth."

"They'd never rat us out," Thea said.

"Well," I said, wincing, "I kind of told them to."

Selly whipped around and looked at me with such a glare,
it was a miracle it didn't melt me on the spot. "You what?"

"I told them not to lie!" I said. "This was something *we*
chose to do—not them. I'm not taking them down with me."

I'd done enough of that, thank you very much. Dragging
Thea—and even Selly—into the Screaming Smackdown had

been the worst part of getting in trouble. I'd hated hurting Thea when she'd done nothing wrong, and I refused to make the same mistake with Mila and Emery.

My phone buzzed again.

Emery: R's here

Mila: We told her you'll be here in a min

Abby: We're at the hotel! Be right up

She didn't text back as my teammates and I raced across the parking lot. Thea swiped her room key in front of the back door, which let us into the hotel. The second my feet hit the carpet, a wave of relief crashed over me. We were back inside!

"At least we're all sweaty and out of breath," I said. "So she'll believe we've been doing laps."

"As long as you act completely normal," Nina said. "And like we've been hanging out and doing the stairs. Definitely not looking at our phones earlier. Otherwise, we would have seen that our friends texted us and said Rebecca was coming over to talk."

We hurried up to my suite, and I let us in.

Rebecca was seated on the couch with Mila, Emery, and Keir. She looked us up and down as we walked over, an eyebrow raised. She'd spread some papers on the coffee table, and it looked like they'd been deep in show talk.

"Sorry we're late!" Nina said.

"I didn't see your texts," I said, my voice high-pitched. "We were going hard."

"And talking," Thea said.

The rest of us nodded.

Nina, Selly, Thea, and I sat down, and I hoped my face wasn't as pink as it felt. Sweat pooled on my lower back, and I would so need a shower after this.

"No worries," Rebecca said, smiling. "I'm glad you kids were hanging out together."

The four of us traded quick smiles, and I caught Mila's eye. *Whew,* I mouthed. She nodded and smiled.

"I was asking Keir, Mila, and Emery how they're feeling about tomorrow," Rebecca said. She adjusted her position so she was sitting cross-legged on the sofa. "How're you all doing?"

"I'm ready," Thea said. "We're doing great!"

But as I tried to pay attention to everyone, the reality started to hit: Ava and Olivia were coming to Saddlehill. Rebecca knew—I mean, she had to, and she hadn't said anything. But I guess she'd decided to wait until after the show to tell us we'd have new riders joining our team soon. *You could be worrying about nothing*, I told myself. Our team could thrive with them on it, and maybe they'd become new friends. All I could do was wait and see.

29

Nightmare

THE NEXT MORNING, I HEADED TO Canterwood in Rebecca's SUV with the rest of my teammates. It was wild that our last day of competition was here already!

"You're all doing so well," Rebecca said. "I'm incredibly proud of you."

"You'll be even more proud when we win!" Selly said, smiling.

Rebecca laughed, flipping on her blinker to turn onto Canterwood's driveway. "It sounds very cliché, but I'm just as pleased to win or lose," she said. "But winning *would* be sweet."

"Yeaaah!" Keir said. "We're all going to go out there and crush it!"

Everyone else in the SUV cheered, and I glanced over at Mila and caught her eye. She smiled at me, and I thought for the eighty-fifth time this morning how cute she looked today. She'd put her hair in Dutch braids and had tied one braid with an orange ribbon and one with a black one.

There was no typical show dress code today, since it was a Halloween classic, as long as we were in proper riding attire, so I'd gone with a graphic tee with a giant pumpkin on the front, and a long-sleeved black shirt underneath. Black breeches brought the whole look together.

Almost everyone else on our team had chosen Halloween-themed clothes too except for Selly. She was dressed in a normal show outfit.

But what Selly was wearing—or not—was the least of my concerns today. Beau and I were one perfect round away from possibly winning this show. And I wanted it more than anything.

"Want to walk the course with me when we get to the stable?" I asked Mila.

"Sure," she said.

"Thea?" I asked my bestie.

"I would, but I have captain stuff first," she said. "You two go ahead, though."

Rebecca stopped the SUV in the parking lot, and we all piled out. As much fun as I was having at Canterwood, I was getting homesick. I missed Foxbury and Saddlehill. But there was something nice about leaving home only to come back later and feel all cozy again.

Together, Mila and I set off to walk the course. The space was peppered with riders as they talked through strategies and made their plans for their rides.

"It looks so cool!" Mila said. "These Halloween vibes are *immaculate*."

"They really are!" The arena decor from the costume contest was still up, and every jump that had been added had some creepy or cute color scheme or addition to it.

"We have to take it all in now," I said, "because once we're out there, we'll be too focused to look closely at the jumps."

Mila nodded. "Definitely."

With that, we started at the beginning of the nine jumps. The first was a vertical wrapped in faux spiderwebs.

"Look," Mila said, giggling. She touched one of the small plastic spiders that had been stuck into the webbing. "My mom has a basketful of these at home. My dad and I like to pick them out and stick them in random places all over the house in October."

I grinned. "I love that."

"My mom will open the fridge and boom, spider by the butter," Mila said. "Go to the bathroom vanity and reach for a towel. Oh, hello, spider."

I laughed. "Okay, I want to come over and hide spiders around your house!"

"Please do! You'll probably think of places my dad and I haven't. It'll be *great*."

"Deal."

We walked to the next vertical, with orange-and-black rails, and then on to a triple-bar oxer with the poles wrapped in shiny purple and black beads.

Up next was an ascending oxer covered in wide ribbons with pumpkins on them. I made a mental note of how tight it would be from the oxer to the first jump of the double combo.

"This part," Mila said. "This is where things get tricky."

"Yup. We'll need to be completely focused and not think

about anything else at this spot. Just making it through the combo."

Both combo jumps were the same, with their black-and-white rails wrapped in tiny skulls. There was nothing here that would scare Beau or make him shy, but there was the added stress of a double combo. I knew our ride had to be perfect.

After the combo, we walked to an orange-and-yellow oxer, then a green-and-orange vertical.

"Last one!" Mila said as we hit the final obstacle.

This oxer was like the first vertical with its spiderwebs. Except this one had little plastic bats stuck in the webs.

Mila and I stood in silence as we counted strides in our heads and mentally went over the course once more.

"Do you feel good about it?" I asked Mila.

She hesitated, then nodded. "I think so. You?"

"I do. While I get Beau ready and take him to our safety check, I'll have time to think about the course more. But I think I've got it."

Slowly, we worked our way back to the first jump and took one more look at the course before leaving the arena.

"We're going to rock this last phase," I said.

"Yes, we are!" She smiled, and I was glad to see she looked

much less nervous now. Jumping gave her anxiety, but she was fighting back against it every time she came out on a jump course.

I opened my mouth to say something, anything about us, but I swallowed it down before I got a word out. *Wait until after the comp,* I reminded myself. I couldn't risk upsetting Mila or ruining the rest of her show with my confession, especially if she was already into Ellie and didn't want to hear what I had to say.

Back in the stable, I led Beau out of his stall and down the aisle toward the crossties.

"You ready for our last class, boy?" I asked him. "We're doing so—"

I froze, stopping Beau mid-stride, as fear made my heart race. Something was wrong.

I turned around to face Beau and walked away from him backward, gently urging him toward me. He came willingly, and I saw it right away.

Beau was *lame.*

"Oh, Beau," I said, squatting next to his left front leg. I ran my hands down his leg and felt heat around his knee. He stood still as I moved around to his other legs, checking to make sure nothing else was wrong.

"What happened, boy?" I asked him, tears pricking my eyes. "I'm so sorry you're hurt."

Gently, I hugged his neck, then slowly turned him around and led him back to his stall. Once he was safely inside, I gave him a wobbly smile. "I'm going to go find Rebecca. I'll be right back!"

Beau blinked at me, which I knew was him giving me the go-ahead, even though the last thing I wanted to do was leave him.

I speed-walked out of the stable and into the main yard, looking around in every direction to find Rebecca. I needed her *now*. Just as I was about to text her, I spotted her walking from one of the other barns toward the nearest arena.

"Rebecca!" I called.

She whirled around to look at me, and I took off at a sprint in her direction.

"What's wrong?" she asked.

"Beau's lame! His knee is warm, and I don't know what happened." It all tumbled out of me in a rush. "I put him in his stall, but I need you to—"

"Take a breath," Rebecca interrupted. She reached over and squeezed my forearm. "Let's go take a look at him."

Together, we headed to the main barn. I tried not to panic, but it was impossible not to. My horse was injured.

"I don't know what happened," I said. "He was fine when I put him up yesterday!"

"It's not your fault, Abby." Rebecca looked over and gave me a sympathetic look. "These things happen. You take *excellent* care of Beau, so please don't blame yourself."

Ugh, it was hard not to.

Back at Beau's stall, Rebecca checked him over and determined that he did have inflammation in his knee.

"We'll have to pull him from the competition, of course," Rebecca said. "He needs rest, and we'll start cold therapy on his leg and see how he does."

"Poor Beau," I said.

"He'll be okay," Rebecca said, closing his stall door. "We'll team up to take the best care of him and get him feeling much better soon."

"Thank you. I know he'll be fine; I just hate to see him hurting."

Rebecca squeezed my shoulder. "You've done all the right

things for him. But as for you, there's no reason not to finish the competition on a different mount."

I stared at Beau as he took a drink. "I don't know," I said. "I feel so guilty."

"Did you ride Beau while he was lame?" Rebecca asked.

"No." I shook my head.

"Did you push him past his limits? Not give him the proper care?"

"No and no," I said.

"Then you shouldn't feel guilty." Rebecca's tone was firm. "Beau's going to be well taken care of, and we brought Wolfie in case we needed a spare mount for something like this. You've ridden him before."

I nodded, thinking of the calm gray gelding. I'd hopped on him before to get experience riding a different mount. And Wolfie was a great horse, but he wasn't Beau. Still, I had no choice but to ride him, or I'd have to scratch.

"Let's go talk to the officials, file the mount substitution paperwork, and get you two ready to go," Rebecca said.

"All right," I said, trying not to let my chin wobble.

It Comes Down to This

A WHILE LATER, I WALKED WOLFIE toward the main arena for our jump class. Rebecca was right—Beau was getting everything he needed, and if I had another horse available to me, which I did, then I owed it to Beau and to myself to finish the competition.

I'd drawn the last riding position of the day, which meant I'd had to bite my nails and watch everyone go before me. It had made for a long day, but it was finally our turn, and I knew exactly what I needed to do. If Wolfie and I got a clear round, we would win. One knocked rail, and Olivia would clinch first place.

I'd taken my time grooming Wolfie and getting to know him again before warming up, and if I couldn't ride Beau, I was glad to ride him.

Thea walked over and patted Wolfie's neck as she looked up at me. "You ready?" she asked.

"I hope so!" I said. "We need to go clear to win."

Thea nodded. "Yup, but what you also need is to have fun. It's your last ride at Canterwood."

I smiled down at her. "I'm going to channel Sasha and Lauren when I'm out there."

"Nah," Thea said, waving one of her hands. "Channel Abby St. Clair. She's more than enough."

That made me all gooey inside. "Theaaa."

"As team captain, you have to listen to me, so there." She winked and stuck out her tongue at me.

The bell sounded, and the loudspeaker crackled on. "Abigail St. Clair on Big Bad Wolf from Foxbury, please enter the arena."

"Good luck!" Thea said.

I nodded at her and took a deep breath. We could do this.

I squeezed my legs against Wolfie's sides, and we entered the arena. He moved into an easy trot and then a canter as I pointed him at the first jump—the spiderweb vertical.

Nine jumps stood between us and victory.

Game on, I thought.

I kept Wolfie at a medium canter as we reached the obstacle. The spiders and webbing didn't make Wolfie hesitate—not even a little bit. He launched himself into the air over the rails and landed neatly on the other side.

As we made our way toward jump two, I counted strides in my head and made sure I didn't let Wolfie gather too much speed. We needed to maintain a steady pace for now. After the combo, I'd let him out.

We made a straight line to the next vertical, and Wolfie leaped over the rails without even coming close to touching them.

Two down, seven to go!

As he cantered toward the triple-bar oxer, Wolfie snorted and tugged on the reins. He wanted to be let out, but now was not the time. I held firm and didn't give him his head, but thankfully he settled down and didn't keep asking for rein.

The ascending oxer came up fast, and we were ready for it! Wolfie jumped easily over the obstacle, and his mane whipped in the wind as he cantered forward.

Anxiety rose in my chest as we neared the first part of the

double combination. This was where we could mess up *every-thing*. There was one stride after the first half of the combo before the second jump, and I needed to be ready to take off soon after we landed.

Don't freak out, I told myself. *Stay calm!*

Wolfie cantered smoothly toward the first combo jump, and I didn't have any more time to be nervous. He tucked his legs under him and launched into the air while I crouched in the two-point position over him. He landed on the other side, took one stride, and we were going up, up, up again for the second half of the double combo.

I took a big breath of relief as we hit the dirt, not even coming close to touching the rail. Now, I didn't want to let myself get too comfortable, because we still had three jumps left. But the scary combo was over!

I gave Wolfie more rein and let him move into a faster canter as we made a sweeping turn and jumped over the oxer.

Two left!

My heartbeat pounded in my ears, nearly drowning out the sounds of Wolfie's hoofbeats as we reached the eighth jump. Wolfie rocked back on his haunches and pushed off with his hind legs, propelling us over the next-to-last obstacle.

One. More.

One more, and we had this!

As we started in a straight line toward the jump, all I could think about was this moment and how my horse was making me so darn proud.

All the noise of people in the stands fell away. I couldn't hear anything but Wolfie's breathing and his hooves pounding the dirt.

At precisely the right second, he launched himself into the air over the spiderweb-and-bat oxer. He was knees to nose as he arched over the oxer. We landed far on the other side, and I pumped my fist in victory as Wolfie cantered away from the jump.

Everyone in the stands was on their feet. We didn't need to wait for the official results. There had been no faults.

WOLFIE AND I WON! Our first blue of the season and it was at Canterwood Crest Academy! Was this real life?!

"GO, ABBY!"

"ABBY! ABBY!"

I let Wolfie sweep around in a large half circle, taking a mini victory lap until I eased him to a trot and then a walk. Tears blurred my vision as I leaned forward in the saddle and squeezed Wolfie's neck.

"We did it!" I told him. "You did great! Thank you so much for helping me today!"

Wolfie snorted, sidestepping and tossing his head. He knew how well he'd done.

I walked him out of the arena, shaking from excitement, and we weren't three feet out of the exit when Thea, Mila, Emery, Keir, Nina, and *Selly* mobbed us.

Thea grabbed Wolfie's reins under his chin and looked up at me, her brown eyes shining. "Abby! You freaking won!"

Everyone else started talking so fast, there wasn't a second for me to say anything. Instead, I grinned and took it all in.

"I knew you could do it!" Mila said. "First place!"

"Way to go, Abby!" Emery cheered, clutching her hands together in front of her.

"You and Wolfie looked so good!" Keir said. "He really came through for you and Beau!"

Nina gave me a small smile. "Congrats, Abby!"

Selly caught my eye and reached up to pat Wolfie's neck. "That was . . ." She paused, and I was sure she was going to be snarky. "A decent ride," she finished.

I'd take it.

"Thank you!" I said. I hopped off Wolfie and loosened his

girth. "I gotta get this champ cooled down, and then go tell Beau! I'm still in shock!"

Thea, Mila, and Emery walked away from the arena with me and Wolfie, and I caught the eyes of Ava and Olivia, who nodded at me from where they stood near the rail. My future *teammates* looked pleased.

31

The Legend

AFTER WOLFIE WAS COOLED OUT, we completed our turnback, where the officials checked him and his tack. We passed, of course, with no issues. And then it became really and truly official.

"Check the results!" Thea said.

I pulled up the website on my phone and grinned.

"It's real!" I said. "I won!"

"Yessss!" Thea said. "You did!"

And our team had come in first, which was glorious.

TEAM NAME/STABLE						
TEAM 1/FOXBURY		DRESS.	SHOW JUMPING		XC	RIDING TOTALS
RIDER	HORSE	SCORE	SCORE			
THEA SONG*	CHAOS GREMLIN	31.00	0.00		0.00	31.00
ABIGAIL ST. CLAIR	BEAU OF MINE/ BIG BAD WOLF	30.00	0.00		0.00	30.00
NINA WILKERSON	ADORE	32.00	4.00		0.00	36.00
MILA BLOOM	CIRCE	33.00	4.00		0.00	37.00
		BEST 3	BEST 3		BEST 3	
		93.00	4.00		0.00	97.00
*DENOTES TEAM CAPTAIN						

Ava and Olivia's team had taken second, and Keir's team had snagged third.

Thea walked with me to the stable to untack and groom Wolfie. Everyone else was off getting their horses packed up and ready to go. Tonight was our last night in the hotel, and we were taking off by seven tomorrow morning to head back to Foxbury and Saddlehill.

Thea helped me get Wolfie cleaned up and in his stall. After I turned him loose inside, I dug a couple of peppermint treats from the bag in my tack trunk. I offered them to him, and he quickly lipped them up and crunched on the hard candies. Then I gave Beau treats and made sure he knew I couldn't have done this without him.

Outside the stable, we ran into Nina and Mila, who were waiting for us to go get our ribbons.

"I'm so glad we won," Nina said. "Ava and Olivia will come to Foxbury knowing who the best riders are."

"Agreed," Thea said.

Selly, Keir, and Emery headed our way, and we walked toward the prize tent together.

When we reached the tent, I looked at the layout of ribbons and almost couldn't believe that one of those was for me. And not just *any* ribbon either. But a blue one. The winning ribbon.

Eric and Mr. Conner were behind the table, handing out ribbons to riders.

"Hi, Abby!" Eric said, smiling. "I've got a shiny blue one for you."

I grinned as he handed it to me and then shook my hand. "You had a wonderful event," Eric said. "We're all proud of you."

"Thank you," I said. "I'm so glad I got to ride here. It's been a bucket list item."

Mr. Conner looked over at me and nodded. "Eric's right. You did great, and you're welcome back anytime. You have an exciting future ahead of you."

"We're looking forward to seeing your journey, Abby," Eric said. "Congratulations!"

I thanked them and tried not to float as my head spun. To have them think I was a good rider with potential? It meant so much to me.

I left the tent while the rest of my team got their ribbons and waited a few steps away, where it was quieter.

I pulled my phone out of my pocket and FaceTimed Dad, hoping he'd answer.

He did on the second ring, and I held my blue ribbon up near my face.

"Guess who won?!" I asked.

Dad punched the air with his free hand. He smiled so wide, and I swear, his eyes got a little teary. "ABBY! That's my girl! I'm so proud of you, honey!"

"Thanks, Dad! My team took first, and Emery's came in third!"

"Wow," Dad said. "That's fantastic! I knew you two would do well. Congratulations, Abby. I hope you're proud of yourself."

"I am. And Beau, too. Oh! I even had to ride a different horse!"

Dad's eyes widened. "What happened?!"

Quickly, I filled him in on the basics.

"I can't wait to hear all the details. I'm sure you're tired now, but when you get back to school, FaceTime me and walk me through all your classes."

"I will," I said, grinning.

We hung up, and I held my ribbon carefully, staring at it. I couldn't wait to show it to Beau!

Back in the stable, I skipped up to Beau's stall and unlatched the door. I let myself inside, and he moseyed over to me, sniffing my hands.

"Look at this," I said, holding out the blue ribbon to him. "Our first individual win of the season, boy. Hopefully, the first of many."

I reached up and pinned it on his halter. "There," I said. "Now you can enjoy it too, while I pack us up."

But before I left the stall, I snapped a picture of Beau with his head high. He looked great in blue, and I couldn't wait to keep adding to our ribbon collection.

I headed for Circe's stall, where I found Mila putting away her horse's grooming kit. I needed to do this now, before I changed my mind.

"Hey," I said. "Do you have a minute?"

Mila nodded. "What's up?"

My palms sweated, and I wiped them on my pants. If I didn't say this now, I never would. "Well, I kind of lied to you," I blurted out.

Mila raised an eyebrow. "About *what*?"

"There's no girl from science class."

Mila frowned. "Then why did you tell me that?"

"I thought my best friends were dumping me," I said. "And I was all caught up in trying to figure out what was going on with them, so I didn't text you back when I should have. And then I got all weird and felt like I couldn't handle *anything* right, so that stupid lie popped out." I swallowed. "I wanted to go to a dance with you more than anything, and I'm so sorry my friendship crisis got in the way."

Mila blinked at me, not saying a word. She shook her head, and her cheeks flushed. "Abby! I thought—oh my god." She rubbed her forehead. "I thought you didn't like me anymore! And I didn't know why! Things had been going so well, and I thought, wow, this girl could one day maybe be my—" Mila stopped, biting on her lower lip.

"Your what?"

Mila's eyes met mine. For a second, I kind of forgot where I was, and all I could see was her. "My . . . *girlfriend.*"

"I—I wanted that too. I *want* that, I mean. I'm so sorry. I should have been honest with you before."

Mila nodded. "Yeah, because you acted like you didn't care about me." She eyed me. "I tried to pretend like I was at least sort of okay at lessons and fine with us being friends, so I didn't make things awkward for everyone."

My eyes welled with tears. "I'm so sorry. Once everything worked out with Thea and Vivi, I knew I needed to talk to you."

"Did you *just* fix things with them?" Mila asked.

"No." I winced a little. "We talked it all out before we left for Canterwood."

Mila swatted my arm. "Why did you wait so long to come to me?"

"I didn't want to cause any drama while the show was happening, because it was a big deal to come here! And you were with Ellie at the dance and—"

"As *friends*, Abby Obviously."

I couldn't help but smile at the nickname, and I sucked in a breath at the *F* word. "Friends? Really?"

"Really," Mila said. "I asked her to dance, as friends,

~ 272 ~

because I thought dancing might help me forget about you. At least for one night."

"Did it work?"

"Not even a little bit. All I could do was keep sneaking glances at you."

I reached out and slid my hand into Mila's. She squeezed my hand, and I tried not to stop breathing. "I saw you with Ellie, and my heart broke. I thought I'd messed up my shot with you if you were into her."

"That's how I felt when you mentioned Science Girl. It was awful."

"Can you forgive me?" I was a little terrified to hear her answer, even though she was still holding my hand.

"Only if you promise to talk to me next time," she said. "And be honest about what's going on."

"I promise," I said, squeezing her hand. "I like you so much, and I won't mess this up."

She grinned. "Good. Because I like you so much too."

Mila's eyes sparkled as she looked at me. So, no, that was not just a thing that happened in cartoons. Eyes could *sparkle*.

I let go of her hand and helped her lay out Circe's travel

boots. I looked up as boots tapped down the aisle, and a young woman with light brown hair and a very familiar face headed in our direction. She looked effortlessly cool in dark jeans tucked into paddock boots and a light pink tee under a brown leather jacket.

"Oh. My. God," I whisper-hissed to Mila, tapping her on the arm. *Repeatedly.*

"What?" She turned around to look, following my open-mouthed gaze. My brain short-circuited.

"No *way*," Mila whispered.

It was Sasha Silver.

The Sasha Silver.

Sasha Freaking Silver was here.

At Canterwood Crest Academy.

AND SHE WAS HEADED TOWARD ME!

"Hi!" Sasha called, giving us a friendly smile.

I stared, unable to remember what words were until Mila elbowed me in the side.

"Hey!" I said.

"Sorry to bother you," she said. "I'm Sasha Silver."

"You—you're not," I said quickly. "Bothering us, I mean! We know you're Sasha Silver!"

She laughed, and her green eyes met mine. "Oh no, my reputation precedes me, huh?"

"Um, only in the best way possible," Mila said. "You're kind of a big deal in the equestrian world."

Sasha waved one of her hands. "Eh, you should see my girlfriend ride. She's got me beat."

I wanted to be like, I know who that is! Heather Fox! But I didn't want to seem like a *stalker*, so I just nodded.

"Anyway, I know you're both busy," Sasha said, "but I'm here for a meeting with Eric and Mr. Conner. Eric was telling me about the winning team, and when he mentioned your name, Abby, I recognized you from your application to my winter clinic."

She did *not* just say that.

"*You* recognized *my* name?" I was going to pass away. Right here. On the spot.

Sasha pulled her phone from her back pocket. "Mm-hmm. Probably because I got two application videos from you."

I frowned. "Two? I only sent one."

Sasha tapped on her phone screen. "I don't think you meant for us to see the first one."

Dread filled my body. What was she talking about?

"Here," Sasha said, handing me her phone. "This is what you emailed us."

I tapped on the video and watched as I rode Beau around the arena, pointing him toward the rail so we could head down to C. . . .

I gasped. *"No."*

No. No. No.

Mila stiffened next to me.

Cold sweat broke out over my body as I froze, staring at the video. I watched in horror as Beau bucked, and I sailed through the air and landed in the dirt.

Blood whooshed in my ears, and I couldn't breathe. There was no question who had done this.

Selly had gotten her revenge. The egging had been a fake-out, meant to throw me off and make me think she was done with me.

Numbly, I handed Sasha her phone.

"Heather and I noticed something odd," Sasha said. "That email came from 'abbyystclair@gmail.com.' And we noticed the other email with your second video was from 'abby' with one *y*."

"My email address only has one *y* in it," I managed to get out. "I never sent that first one."

Sasha frowned. "I figured. I'm sorry someone did that to you."

Do not cry in front of Sasha, I told myself. But my winter clinic dreams were over.

"Thanks for telling me," I said, unable to look her in the eye. "I'm sure you have a lot of applicants to go through."

"We do," she said. "And if you're telling me this isn't the video you want us to judge you on, then . . ." Sasha tapped on her phone again before looking back at me. "It's deleted. Heather and I will make our decision based on your *correct* submission video."

"Really?!" My heart thudded so hard, I was sure Sasha and Mila could hear it. "You'd do that?"

"Of course," Sasha said. "We want to choose fairly. And what someone did to you wasn't fair."

"Thank you *so* much," I said.

"No problem." Sasha smiled. "I'll be in touch with our decision."

She headed back down the aisle. Before she got too far, she turned back around. "Oh, and Abby, if you have trouble with whoever sent that and you need to talk about it, you have my email." She tossed us one last smile and disappeared down the aisle.

I turned to Mila. "Did that just—"

"Happen? It did!" She grabbed both of my hands. "Selly tried to ruin your shot, and she failed!"

"And it made me meet Sasha! Wait until Selly hears *that*!"

We giggled until we were breathless.

"C'mon," I said. "Let's get packed up."

Mila nodded. "We can finish Circe first, then work on Beau's stuff."

"Perfect," I said. "Coming to Canterwood was great, and it was my dream to see this place, but I'm ready to go home. We have a *lot* to do."

Acknowledgments

Huge thanks to my agent, Josh Getzler, for all your cheerleading and unwavering support. And thank you so much to Jon Cobb and the rest of the HG Literary team.

Alyson Heller, thank you a million times for making this book so much fun and so sparkly to write! Jessi Smith, I greatly appreciate all your wisdom and editorial help.

To the rest of my S&S team—thank you so, so much to Valerie Shea, Chel Morgan, Karin Paprocki, Valerie Garfield, Kaitlyn San Miguel, Olivia Ritchie, Kristin Gilson, and Anna Jarzab. Lana Dudarenko, you're the best cover artist a girl could ask for! Thank you to Rebekkah Ross for bringing the audiobooks to life! And thank you to the Simon Kids social media team for being amazing!

Hugs and thanks to my family—Mom, Dad, Jason, and Lorrie—for all their support while I wrote this book. And to Grandma, Kerry, and the rest of my family who all cheer me on.

The biggest of hugs to Julia Hezel—how did I get so lucky to be your best friend? Shanna Alderliesten, my go-to horse-girl friend, thank you for all of the notes! I cannot wait to visit one day and hang out. Misty Wilson, I'd be completely lost without you to talk to about *everything*. Emma Goldstein, thank you for screaming in my DMs as I teased this book, and thank you, Marissa Eller, for the most supportive texts. Jen Kurtyak, your immaculate Halloween vibes definitely influenced this book.

I'd be so lonely without my writer group! Everyone in the Trifecta is truly wonderful. Special thanks to Tess Sharpe for bringing us together.

I greatly appreciate the support from booksellers, librarians, and teachers. Endless thanks to Kendall at Porter Square Books and Jennifer Rummel.

Thank you so much to all the United States Pony Clubs who have embraced Saddlehill! And thanks to the Interscholastic Equestrian Association riders. So many thanks to Maggie at Hollins University for your endless support!

Lastly, thank you again to my readers. You're truly the best.

FIVE GIRLS. ONE ACADEMY. AND SOME SERIOUS DRAMA.

CANTERWOOD CREST

by Jessica Burkhart

TAKE THE REINS
BOOK 1

CHASING BLUE
BOOK 2

BEHIND THE BIT
BOOK 3

TRIPLE FAULT
BOOK 4

BEST ENEMIES
BOOK 5

LITTLE WHITE LIES
BOOK 6

RIVAL REVENGE
BOOK 7

HOME SWEET DRAMA
BOOK 8

CITY SECRETS
BOOK 9

ELITE AMBITION
BOOK 10

**SCANDALS,
RUMORS, LIES**
BOOK 11

**UNFRIENDLY
COMPETITION**
BOOK 12

CHOSEN: **INITIATION** **POPULAR** **COMEBACK** **MASQUERADE**
SUPER SPECIAL BOOK 13 BOOK 14 BOOK 15 BOOK 16

JEALOUSY **FAMOUS** **HOME FOR CHRISTMAS:**
BOOK 17 BOOK 18 SUPER SPECIAL

EBOOK EDITIONS AVAILABLE
ALADDIN ❧ SIMONANDSCHUSTER.COM/KIDS

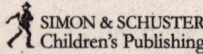 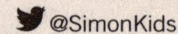